D.J. ADAMSON

INTO THE STORM

INTO THE STORM

D. J. ADAMSON

HORATIO PRESS

MYSTERY-SUSPENSE-SCIENCE FICTION

979-8-9886593-0-3

Also By

Lillian Dove Mystery Series
Admit to Mayhem
Suppose
Let Her Go
With a Vengeance (2021)

Science Fiction / Paranormal
Approaching Storm
(Prequel to Into the Storm)

Psychological Thriller
At the Edge of No Return

For Luanne
A mermaid in all the possibilities of mermaids. Inner and outer universes are same, imagination and reality, all reflections of whom we may really be.

"Soul of all souls, life of all life- you are That.
Seen and unseen, moving and unmoving - you are That.
The road that leads to the City is endless;
Go without head and feet
and you'll already be there.
What else could you be? - you are That."
- Rumi

"Riders on the storm...Into
this world we're thrown."
- The Doors

CHAPTER ONE: JACK CAHILL

August 7, 1989, MIDNIGHT.

ITS head was much larger than its body.

ITS skin, gray like the cold stone of the cave. IT sat next to a small campfire across from him.

"Pitts? Diddleman?" Jake shouted, seeing the hooded shirts Diddleman and Pitts had been wearing on the ground. He glanced around his surroundings and spotted another piece of clothing-- sky-blue, like the blouse his sister wore when she was taken. The material showed brilliant on the top of a dirty, rotten-smelling debris pile.

ITS large, oval-shaped black eyes stared over at him. A sound came from a hole where its mouth should have been.

SQUEAL!

IT wasn't human. Or Jake didn't think it was human. Actually, he wasn't sure what IT was.

"What have you done with my friends?!" Jake screamed, struggling against the cords biting into him. "Where are my mom and sister?"

ITS mouth opened again as if IT was trying to speak.

IT garbled loudly, "*DAAIDDIDIDAWOOOO?*"

Then, suddenly, IT rose, small, torso long, legs small, and stepped toward him.

"Don't you come near me," Jake threatened. But he wasn't sure what he would do if it did. Jake had nothing to protect himself. He could barely move against the restraints. And his legs ached as if he'd been standing for a very long time.

IT came close, assaulting his senses with dirt, rot, and decay. Also, a metallic smell itched his nose. Looking down, he noticed the blood smeared on its gray feet. Not feet exactly. Clubs. Hard. They thumped the stone as IT came closer.

"Pitts?!" Jake yelled again. He was frightened for his friends. Terror weakened his legs even more to where now he sagged against his restraints. And when his appeal went unanswered, with not nearly as loud a voice but with the hope his friends were nearby, could hear him, and were still all right, he called, "Diddleman?!"

Only a tiny echo returned his voice. Tears welled in his eyes. Then, unashamedly, not because he thought she was near, here in the cave with him, but because he wished to turn back time, return to her protective arms, he whimpered, "Mom?!"

IT raised its hand, fingers long. Its index finger was longer than its middle finger. Much longer. Inhumanly long. IT pointed the finger toward Jake.

"DAAIDDIDIDDAWOOOOO. JAKKEEEEE."

Jake was sure he was about to be killed.

CHAPTER TWO: SHERIFF BOGGS

August 7, 1989, 1 a.m.

"Catch your breath, Walter."

Walter's mouth gaped. His lungs sucked air, bellows trying to ignite an icy fire. Rain dripped from his forehead onto his t-shirt, the wet clinging like another layer of skin.

Sheriff Roger Boggs of Circlegold County found a blanket to throw over him. On last look outside, he'd seen that a light rain was falling, but, he reasoned, this boy got caught in a storm.

What was he doing out so late? Boggs was pretty damn sure the boy's parents weren't aware of his late-night activities. He asked, "Is that all you were wearing out in this rain?"

The kid looked at himself and then checked around as if he had something else, but it was missing.

So far, Boggs had listened to five minutes of babble. And so far, there was no making heads or tails out of what the kid was trying to tell him.

"This kid's pulling our leg." Officer Hayworth of the Pinkerton City Police pulled off his yellow rain slicker and shook it out onto the floor before finding the back of a chair to hang it on. He stood next to Walter, his hands clenched to his hips, fingers inches away from his gun as if the kid posed a threat.

Boggs ignored Hayworth. "Walter, who did you say was with you?"

"Jake Cahill," Walter stammered. "And Oliver Pitts." He drew in a large breath and exhaled. "I'm telling you the truth, Sheriff."

Officer Hayworth should have delivered Walter to the city police's threshold. Police Chief Purvis Moore held jurisdiction over the citizens of Pinkerton. When Moore found out his officer delivered Walter to Boggs' office, he'd be pissed. No more than pissed, Boggs guessed. He'd shove his foot in the stirrup of his outrage saddle and mount his high horse.

Of course, Hayworth wasn't innocent. He'd brought Walter Forester into the Sheriff's station, knowing the possible consequences.

And yet, Boggs thought, he did. Why?

Hayworth said, "He kept saying he needed to talk to Sheriff Boggs. Hells-bells, I didn't know what to do. I didn't want to wake up the Chief. Not at this time of night. Not if the kid were going to tell him he wouldn't talk to anyone but you."

Boggs noticed the slight shiver moving through Hayworth's thin stature. The trembling wasn't from being out in the storm but from the unnerving possibility that he may have made the wrong decision.

Pinkerton Police and the County Sheriff's Office were located in the old Pinkerton City Hall. Unusual in more populated cities, but smaller towns learned to survive by moderation.

But different jurisdictions sometimes blurred authority in people's minds at such close quarters. They would enter on the Sheriff's side through the western door instead of the City Police side at the eastern entrance. Double-glass doors in the middle of the 100-year-old building opened to the Circlegold County Museum. The doors were generally only open for elementary school children on a special field trip day.

Jurisdictions did sometimes legitimately cross in emergencies. Like when the tornado hit. When the twister opened its jaws onto Pinkerton and chewed its way through neighborhoods barely a week ago, no one checked who worked for whom. All personnel of both city and county were called into action.

However, so far, Officer Hayworth's bringing Walter into his office didn't present itself as an emergency.

Boggs looked to the boy sitting in front of him. Walter Forrester was a short, stocky kid somewhere around fifteen years old. He had a square head and bad acne. Any reputation made for himself so far in life came from his position on the wrestling team. Boggs wasn't sure how he'd gotten the nickname Diddleman but considered it a name reserved for those buddies of his age.

Boggs did not know Walter that well, but everyone in Pinkerton knew each other to a degree. Boggs knew Walter's best hanging-around friends were Jake Cahill and Oliver Pitts. So, hearing their names connected to this possible ruckus did not surprise him.

"Blast it," Hayworth cussed, continuing his rant. "I told him he should tell Chief Moore about all this first, but he wouldn't hear it."

Skinny, to the point of almost non-existent hipbones, Officer Hayworth readjusted his duty belt and gun.

Hayworth reminded Boggs of one of those little hairless Chihuahuas. The type that perceives themselves as a Rottweiler but never quite measures up.

"Damn kid said he could only tell you," Hayworth went on. "And well, blast it, the park is your jurisdiction." Hayworth finished with, "Even so, the Chief's not going to like me being here and not there." He sniffed and pulled at his equipment belt. "I should call Chief Moore."

"Do as you see fit," Boggs responded, only half listening. His concentration was on Walter, bulging eyes, frozen wide, staring straight at him. Boggs thought that the kid would bolt from his chair if a door banged shut.

What kind of trouble had these kids got themselves into?

"Do you think you can start over from the beginning?" Boggs said.

"It's got them," Walter mewed.

"Got who?" Hayworth spat.

"Jake. Pitts."

"Who's got them?" Hayworth demanded.

"The alien," Walter emphasized the word alien.

Hayworth pursed his lips and sneered. "This is that kid Cahill's doing. He's a known storyteller. He tried to pull one over on me when he reported his parents' home burgulared after the tornad'er hit. As if we in law enforcement don't have enough to do. This one here," he pointed to Walter, "he was in on it."

Walter twisted around in his chair. "It was bur...gal...whatever you said."

Hayworth sniffed with annoyance. Exasperated, his hands flapped back to his hips. "As if a tornad'er wasn't bad enough. All us in the force, trying to keep the peace, are faced with...."

"Why would we write stuff on the walls of Jake's house?" Walter objected. "We told you it wasn't us."

Hayworth snarled, "If I could figure out what makes a kid tick, I'd be rich."

Boggs wanted to get back to why Walter was in his office. "Start again from the very beginning. Why did the three of you go to Eagles tonight?"

Walter's full attention came immediately back to Boggs. "We didn't."

"Then why'd you tell me you were at Eagles?" Officer Hayworth snapped.

This time Walter didn't bother twisting around to Officer Hayworth. He explained to Boggs, "You see, Jake's dad was missing. We found him at the hospital. Or Jake did. Pitts and I didn't go into the room. Just Jake. Only, everyone said it wasn't his dad. But Jake ought to know his dad. Right?"

He did not wait for a response. "Jake said his dad was hurt really bad in a fire."

Walter slid forward on his chair. "When we went back to the hospital the second time because..."

"Second time?" Hayworth interrupted. "Hells-fire. Do you kids think the hospital has nothing more to do than..."

"Officer," Boggs interrupted. "Let the boy tell it."

Hayworth pivoted his head and sniffed with contempt. "I ain't stopping him. Go ahead, boy."

Walter continued. "Dr. Potter took Jake's dad out of the hospital because his dad told Jake something he wasn't supposed to. Something about Eagle's Nest."

Walter began coughing.

"Take another breath," Boggs instructed. "Relax."

"Slow the heck down," Officer Hayworth demanded. Sniffed. "How're we supposed to understand you if you're talking a mile a minute?"

"What is Eagle's Nest?" Boggs asked.

Walter shrugged. "I don't know exactly. Jake said it was a place only he and his dad knew about. Jake said his dad was trying to tell him where to find his mother and sister. You know, they're missing, too? I bet that alien kidnapped them."

Boggs looked to Hayworth. City would handle missing persons. "Do you know anything about Bill Cahill missing?"

"First, I'm learning about it," Hayworth sniffed.

"He is missing," Walter insisted. "I'm being legit, Sheriff. Jake's dad was trying to find Jake's mother and sister."

Hayworth sniffed. "Lots of people were taken to nearby hospitals after the tornad'er hit." He mumbled, "Bunch of baloney."

Walter said, "Jake said he knew the place his dad was talking about. It was a place where they used to go fishing. That's why we were at Eagles."

"In the dark?" Hayworth scoffed.

"Stanley, let the boy talk," Boggs warned. If the man did not quit interrupting, he would never get the story straight.

"We had flashlights," Walter returned, "and believe me, I wanted to wait until morning. But Jake wouldn't hear it." He swiveled a half-twist toward Officer Hayworth. "Finding Jake's family was more important than it being dark. We weren't afraid."

Officer Hayworth shifted his attention away from Walter and pulled up his equipment belt.

Walter said, "Jake said there was no trail to the bird's nest. It's like a secret place. He thought he could find it. Only, we got kind of lost in the dark." His words came faster with the telling, "Jake wasn't so sure anymore. And then something attacked us."

"What do you mean, attacked you?" Boggs questioned.

Walter itched his head and circled the answer. "It'd been following us. I'm pretty sure of that. I figured it was Templeton."

"Ted Templeton?" Boggs was surprised with another name coming into the story.

Walter nodded. "Teddy's always following Jake around."

He suddenly jolted up high in his chair. "But then, we saw it."

"Saw what?" Officer Hayworth asked anxiously. He was leaning over now, not wanting to miss a word of what Walter was telling.

Walter's eyes grew glassy. "It was eating a deer."

"Coyote, probably," Officer Hayworth sniffed with a note of authority.

"It wasn't a coyote," Walter cried. "It isn't an animal." He stared at Boggs, daring him to call him a liar. "It isn't human, either. Pitts said so, and Pitts's smart."

He gulped. "It wasn't big, and it had long arms. Like one of those pictures Pitts has of aliens. It came toward us, and then it must have got scared because it ran off. We followed it."

"How'd you follow it so easily in the dark," Hayworth challenged.

Walter retaliated. "We followed it easy because it was squealing."

"Squealing?" Hayworth asked, "You mean like a pig?"

"Maybe," Walter replied. He looked off beyond Boggs as if trying to hear it again. He shook his head. "No, not like a pig." He said to Boggs, "It's hard to explain."

"Don't dwell on it right now," Boggs said. "Continue with what happened next."

"We came out of the woods into a clearing. That's when we found the burned house." He rushed on, "I thought right away about Jake's dad. Jake said he was burned real bad. And I thought this must be the nest." Walter closed his eyes. "Eagles Nest. Although not really a nest."

He kept his eyes shut, again as if he had time-jumped to that very moment. As if he was seeing it in his mind. He. whispered. "It was standing by the body."

"Body? What body?" Officer Hayworth said.

Walter whispered, "A girl."

Hayworth was so stunned by the response his equipment belt almost fell to his knees.

"I think the alien killed her," Walter told Boggs. "Her neck was ripped open, and you could see her intestines in her stomach."

He retched. "I'm going to be sick."'

"Take a deep breath," Boggs advised, wanting to keep the kid at the moment. "Did you recognize the girl?"

This time Hayworth gagged. Boggs grabbed the wastepaper basket from under his desk. "In here," he demanded of Hayworth.

Walter's voice stayed low. He shook his head. "It wasn't Jake's sister. Shilo's hair is red. This girl had..." his voice trembled, and his body shivered as if he'd suddenly felt a cold breeze.

A tear slipped from the corner of Walter's eye. "You need to find them, Sheriff."

"Don't worry. I will." Boggs stood up. "Let's get you home."

Walter bulked. "I'm not done telling you."

Boggs sat back down. "There's more?"

"We were coming to get the police," Walter went on, "but it showed up again. This time we saw Chewbacca running with it."

Hayworth stiffened, sniffed, "Didn't I tell you, Sheriff? He's making up a bunch of nonsense. Aliens, phooey. He's telling what he saw in some movie." He put the wastebasket down and then moved over to the doorway as if finished with the conversation.

Boggs heard him mutter, "Good thing I didn't get the Chief up for this drivel."

"Chewbacca is Jake's dog," Walter explained. "I don't know how Chewbacca got there. Jake told us he disappeared along with his mom."

Walter looked directly at Boggs. "I saw Pitts drop to the ground. It must have done something to him. And then, something hit me on the back of the head. When I woke up, both Jake and Pitts were gone."

His chin quivered. "I know I should have stayed to look for them. I know I shouldn't have come back without them. But I didn't know what else to do."

"You did the right thing," Boggs assured Walter. "Let me take it from here."

CHAPTER THREE

Boggs grappled with the ringing phone and brought it to his ear. "What can I do for you, Purvis?"

"I heard there was an incident at Eagles." The voice paused as if waiting for Boggs to respond.

Hayworth had left only a couple of minutes ago. Boggs had him drive Walter home. Did Hayworth redecide and call his boss as soon as he got in his cruiser?

"I heard kids pulled a practical joke on the Forester kid. And now the joke's stretched to you." Moore laughed.

"Nah," Boggs said. "I'm heading home and looking forward to hitting the hay."

"I hear you. I'm done in, too. I'm heading that way myself."

Boggs glanced at the time. He didn't need to look out to the city police lot to see that the City Chief's SUV was gone. Boggs would have bet it hadn't been in the lot since well after six o'clock. And he would have bet double Purvis Moore was calling from bed.

"Is that why you're calling, Purvis?" Boggs asked. " Just to see if the kids pulled one over on me?"

Moore didn't answer.

Boggs said, "Walter said Bill Cahill's missing. I was surprised to hear it."

Moore said, "There's no missing person's report on him.

Boggs added, "Walter also said Jake's mom and sister are missing."

Moore begged off the question. "Good thing school's starting in a couple of weeks. We need to keep these kids busy and off the streets."

"The way Walter told it," Boggs continued, "Oliver Pitts and Jake Cahill and he went up to Eagles tonight because they found Bill

Cahill gravely injured at the hospital. Bill told Jake where he could find his missing mother and sister."

"So, are you buying what the kid says? Are you going to Eagles to check out the story? This time of night?"

Boggs hadn't made that decision yet. If the two boys had played a prank on Walter, sending deputies to check out the story was a waste of time and resources.

"I'd get some sleep if it were me. This yarn smells like a prank, Roger." Moore guffawed. "Let me know if you hear anything more."

"You'll be first on my list." Boggs ended the call.

As soon as he hung up the phone, Boggs dialed Pinkerton General Hospital. When the operator picked up, he asked, "Can you connect me to someone who can check for a patient?"

"I can check that for you," the person answered.

"I'd like to know if you have a patient by the name of Bill or William Cahill."

"And you are?"

"This is Sheriff Boggs."

"I thought that sounded like you, Sheriff. This is Kalee Mitchell. I am on night duty tonight. You're up awfully late."

"Sorry about the hour."

"Not to worry, that's my job."

Boggs heard fingers tapping on keys. "No, sorry. No one here by that name."

"Any Cahills, admitted?"

"No, sir."

"Thanks." He hung up. Scratched his head. Why would Walter have mentioned Jake Cahill's father in the hospital if it weren't true? Something easily checked.

Boggs called up and told the night dispatcher where to reach him if needed. He emphasized the word needed. Then he walked out of the station and got into his SUV.

The rain had stopped, but the air lay heavy with moisture. Boggs glanced at his watch. Almost three a.m. and still stifling hot. He sat with the windows down, waiting for the air conditioner to push out the oppressive heat. He replayed all of what Walter had told him. None of it made sense. Was it a big hoax on Walter?

And the deer? Had poachers been out hunting? Did they feel their chance of being caught minimalized due to the park closures? Of course, hunting was not allowed in the park. And deer season outside the park was still two months away. Yet, there were some whose fingers always itched to kill something.

None of that explained the dead girl. Was someone else brought in on the joke? A girlfriend, maybe? And who did they get to play the alien?

Then there was Moore calling minutes after Hayworth left. Hayworth probably called his boss to keep his butt clean. No doubt about that. And Moore's calling him was Moore's way of letting Boggs know he was fully aware of what went on in the Sheriff's office. But why hadn't Moore waited until morning to get in his jab?

And why was Purvis so sure it was a joke? Hayworth calling Purvis, risk waking his boss in the middle of the night was one thing. Moore accepting Hayworth's opinion of what was going on weighted heavier on the ain't- gonna-happen- meter.

Boggs gave a heavy sigh. He knew he would not get a lick of sleep unless he checked out some of Walter's story.

He flipped on the car's turn signal, then took a left instead of a right toward home in the direction of Highway 99 and Eagles Park."

CHAPTER FOUR

The entrance to Eagles Park off Highway 99 was a speedometer distance of seven miles from Pinkerton.

The park was approximately a thousand acres, including a lake, three major campgrounds, and hiking trails. It was open nearly year-round, only closed during the deep freeze of winter when the snow levels could reach well over four feet, and the wind chill factor could drop the temperature gauge below zero degrees. This time of year, two weeks before school started, the park was widely available to hikers, campers, and those who wanted a cool dip to take off the heat.

Driving to the park, Boggs reflected on the recent death of one of his deputies. The day before the storm hit, a park visitor discovered Deputy Wilcox with his own knife stuck bolster-deep into his chest like a Japanese warrior committing Hari Kari. The medical examiner called it the way it appeared, suicide. However, suicide still didn't set well with Boggs. Wilcox had been up for a pay raise. And he was planning to get married in the Fall. Not the type of events that would plague a man into taking his own life.

Against protests from Medical Examiner Dr. Cletus Potter and Park Deputy Elizabeth Warner, the lake area remained closed until Boggs officially signed off on the investigation.

Deputy Warner said she understood Boggs's need for answers but argued people expected their summer plans not to be disrupted. Instead, she said people needed an outlet, especially after the devastation from the storm. She was supported by Potter, arguing there was no evidence of foul play.

Boggs was a man who respected evidence. And Potter was right. The only fingerprints, DNA, and weapon discovered were Wilcox's. So if it was a crime, it was by someone who knew to cover his bases. But what had Wilcox got into that would make someone want to kill him?

Boggs slowed next to the patrol car to keep people out of the lake area. He found the park deputy's head thrown back with his mouth wide open.

Boggs honked. The deputy jumped as if a bullet had whizzed past his ear.

"I take it that it's been quiet," Boggs called over.

Park Deputy Mike Connor rolled down his window. "Just resting my eyes," he grinned. "Nothing is going on. Not even a damn deer around."

"Keep your eyes open," Boggs said. "A report came in tonight. Two kids are missing."

"What kids?" Connor said.

"Oliver Pitts and Jake Cahill."

"Who reported them missing?"

"Walter Forester."

Deputy Connor grunted. "Are we putting a search out for them?"

"We'll give it until morning. But, if you spot the boys, call dispatch, and then take their butts home. Tell them I'll expect them in my office first thing tomorrow morning."

"What'd they do?" Connor asked.

"Nothing more than being teenagers with too much time on their hands." He hoped he was right.

Walter said the boys took the Summit Trail from the RV park, but it was too late to wake those campers without a sufficient reason. Plus, if the two boys were not already home in bed, his best bet would be finding them down by the lake, getting a good laugh out of their hoax. And or taking a cool midnight swim. Hell, he thought, with Deputy Connor snoozing on the job, they could have walked right past him.

He considered calling the Pitts' house to see if the boys had shown up, but he thought he would look around first. There was no reason to get someone else out of a good night's sleep if it wasn't necessary. He could always call them tomorrow and report what the boys had been up to in the middle of the night.

He kept his eyes open for movement as he looped around the picnic area and on down to the lake. A long, cool swim sounded rather good. He parked where he could overlook the dock. He scrutinized the water's surface. No heads of boys swimming. Maybe they hadn't made their way here yet.

He switched off his headlights and rolled down the window. He'd wait a while. Then, opening the cubby, he pulled a cigarette out of the package he stashed there. Lighting up, he inhaled deeply.

He was tired. Needed sleep. His days had been getting longer, not shorter. It'd been a week since the tornado hit Pinkerton, and people were still at a loss on how to pick up their lives and move on. People were displaced from their homes. Services were still out. And the weather forecasters were falling over themselves, offering maps, statistics, and warnings of other potential storms heading this way.

A three-quarter moon muted by clouds created an inky blurring of lines between space and shadow, river and shore. Boggs knew this area of the park beyond his job. As a kid, he'd played in the playground. Picnicked with his family at the wooden tables. On weekends, he and his dad went out to catch Walpole. And one moon-filled night, parked after a date to the movies, he got Connie Lou Miller to let him get to third base.

He drew in another lungful of tobacco. Exhaled.

Deputy Park Manager Elizabeth Warner said those who had lost their homes were coming to camp until they could get their lives together. However, tried and true hikers undaunted by the storm or future tornado warnings continued, drawn back to the trails. Elizabeth just called him again yesterday, asking when he planned to open the lake.

She argued, "Roger, you aren't responsible for not seeing the warning signs. None of us did. Denver Wilcox didn't seem depressed. His death came as a shock to all of us." She said, "Suicide is like that. No one can know what's going on in another person's mind."

He knew she was right. And he had promised to release the closure in twenty-four hours. She would be expecting his call in the morning.

Drawing in deeply, the end of his cigarette burned red in the darkness of the SUV's cab. And the thought of a teenage hoax started getting under his skin. Everyone liked a good prank, but the timing was everything. Stirring up a story like Walter told him was not what anyone needed right now. He planned to visit all three families and talk with the boys and parents as soon as possible.

Boggs glanced across the lake. Walter implied that Ted Templeton was involved. The thought of Ted triggered the memory of Teddy sitting on the opposite side of the bank when they were investigating Deputy Wilcox's death.

There was no confusing Teddy with someone else. He was older than the other boys by about two years. He usually wore a baseball cap from being cursed with early adult balding. Was Teddy somehow involved in Jake and Oliver's prank on Walter? Walter said he thought Teddy was following them. Had the boys talked him into pretending to kidnap them?

Teddy was physically challenged. He was almost as tall as Boggs but pencil-thin. But Walter said the person playing the alien was small.

Drops of rain hit his windshield. Heat and rain. A murky mix.

He gave his cigarette another couple of hits and then tossed it out the window. "Hell," he thought. "I'm a fool to be sitting here waiting for these boys to show up."

He punched on the headlights and gave the surface of the lake and the surrounding area another examination. He continued to keep an eye out as he backed up and left.

CHAPTER FIVE

Too tired to walk the few steps to his bedroom, Boggs removed his duty belt and gun and placed them on the coffee table. He put his cell phone next to them, hoping it wouldn't ring.

He picked up the framed photo of his wife Lacy and his little girl Laura. Laura had only been two at the time of the picture. Boggs named his daughter after his sister and promised her the first moment he held her in his arms that he would protect her. And that while the world could be challenging at times, he would make sure she understood that what someone else said was not always true.

He smiled at how similar mother and daughter were. Twins of each other, both had blonde hair and hazel eyes. Lacy said she always wished for blue eyes, and she hoped Laura would take after him, his eyes bluest of blues. And she complained how she could not tame her hair. It was too curly. Boggs answered her by saying her eyes were almost golden in the sunlight like gems. And he would remind her that he fell in love with her "untamed nature." Not her hair, but her unruly spirit. She kept his world interesting. She made each day exciting.

So long ago, he thought.

He failed both of them in keeping his promise. Seventeen years ago, state patrol found their car on Highway 99, empty. Their bodies were never discovered.

He kissed each face beneath the glass and placed the photograph back.

He resisted glancing at his watch. Seeing the time would only make him feel more exhausted. He hoped to take a couple of hours before he needed to head back to the office.

His eyes closed without bidding. Yet sleep alluded him. Instead, he thought of his father, who had a heart attack while shopping in a sporting goods store for the new fishing pole he had his eye set on. He claimed he was going to fish every day if he wanted. He died a month after retirement.

Boggs groaned with the irony. His father never got the chance to glimpse what it might mean to truly live, taking the day as the day comes, not as others dictate.

The fear he might suffer the same result terrified him.

His cell phone rang.

His first thought was that Deputy Connor had found the boys. It was dispatch. The operator stated she received a call from Mathew Pitts. Mr. Pitts reported he awakened to discover his son missing.

CHAPTER SIX

Boggs punched in the number dispatch gave him.

A voice picked up on the first ring.

"Matt? Sheriff Boggs here."

"Sorry about the late-night call," Mathew Pitts said, excusing for the very early hour."

"No problem, Matt."

"Katherine got up to use the bathroom, and she thought she saw the light on in Oliver's room. Jake Cahill and Walter Forester were staying with Oliver tonight. The room was empty." Boggs heard Katherine Pitts speak in the background. "Yes," Matt confirmed what she'd said, "they went up to Oliver's room about ten last night."

Now, Boggs glanced at his watch. Almost four in the morning. He feared what was coming. "Are you sure they didn't come home and decide to go back out?"

"Come home?" Matt said, "They never left as far as we're aware." He paused. "Hold it, what are you saying? Are you telling me you knew the boys weren't home?"

Boggs mentally kicked himself. As soon as Hayworth drove Walter home, he should have notified the Pitts family. A late hour or not. But then, he figured the boys would be home by now. Boggs didn't like worrying someone until he knew for a fact there was something to stress over.

Damn it still. Right was right, no matter the day or hour. His responsibility was to Matt and Katherine Pitts and the Cahill family.

Boggs explained, "I spoke with Walter Forester a couple of hours ago."

"A couple of hours ago?" Matt's voice rang with unease.

"He told me he, Jake, and Oliver had been over at Eagles Park. I take it you knew nothing of the boys going there?"

"No," Matt answered. "What the hell are they doing there?"

"Where? What is he saying?" Katherine had come closer to her husband, or she was no longer afraid to awaken an empty house.

Boggs said, "Walter came into the office late tonight and told me a story about an incident that happened to the boys at the park. I must tell you, Matt. I would have called you straight away if I'd thought any of it was true. I felt sure the other two boys were playing a prank on Walter." Again, he glanced at his watch. "If the boys still aren't home, well, there may have been more truth in what he told me than I understood at the time."

Matt returned, his voice angrily raised, "What did he tell you?"

Again, Boggs heard Katherine in the background.

Matt answered his wife. "He says Walter told him Jake and Oliver were at Eagles."

"At this time of night? In this weather?" Katherine shouted. "That's ridiculous." Then panic filled her voice, "What are those boys doing at the park?"

A clatter sounded in Boggs' ear as if someone had dropped the phone. Then Matt came back on the line. "They're not upstairs, Sheriff. I don't know what to tell you. Walter was spending the night. If he told you the boys went to the park, then that is where they most likely went."

Boggs then gave Matt an overview of the story. Matt agreed it sounded far-fetched. Like the boys were playing a joke on Walter. But, after Matt relayed what Boggs said to Katherine, she cried, "I want to know where they are. Now."

After the call ended, Boggs didn't spend any time contemplating what to do next. He called Dispatch, ordering, "I want a full search team. Call in those on this morning's duty roster and those on tonight's. Have Deputy Standwick set up a Central Command in the RV camping lot. I am a half-hour out."

He went straight away into the bathroom and threw cold water on his face—no time to shave. "Better get this right, this time," he warned his reflection. He couldn't believe he'd underestimated what Walter was trying to tell him. Simply by calling the Pitts, getting them out of what they thought was a safe night's sleep, he could be hours ahead. Possibly found them already. He glared at his reflection. "If something's happened to those boys, it'll be on you."

He punched on the warning lights in the car but left off the siren. First stop, the Forester home.

The Forester house was dark. Why wouldn't it be? They are probably just as uninformed as Matt and Katherine unless Walter woke them and told them what was going on. But if so, why didn't the Foresters call the Pitts?

Boggs knew Douglas Forester drank too much. A good reason why Walter may not have awakened his parents after Officer Hayworth dropped him home.

Walter's mother, Eunice Forester, unable to fix her husband's drinking problem, concentrated most of her efforts at the local Baptist Church. This morning, her hair looked newly permed, and she was wearing a robe that reached the floor. She pulled the collar higher around her throat. "What are you doing here so early in the morning, Sheriff?"

"Sorry about the time, Eunice, but I need to speak to Walter."

Eunice's eyes widened with concern. "Why, in the devil would you be looking for Walter? He's not here. He's staying over with Oliver Pitts tonight."

Not knowing teenagers' whereabouts was not a new phenomenon, but Boggs thought it was funny that Eunice Forester hadn't heard her son come home. She may not have gotten up to confront Walter about where he'd been, but Boggs didn't think Eunice wasn't aware of what went on in her house.

Boggs said, "I think you'll find him in bed, Eunice. I had Officer Hayworth drop Walter here shortly after midnight."

"What time is it now?"

Boggs checked the time. "It's four-twenty-three."

"Is he in trouble? Did Walter do something?"

Boggs assured her. "Walter's not in trouble. On the contrary, he can help me."

A nasal snort sounded from inside the house. Boggs thought that Doug Forester was on the couch when Walter was dropped off. Again, a good reason Walter must have tip-toed his way inside.

Eunice still seemed confused. "I didn't hear him come home. But, if you say you had him dropped off here, then he must be. Let me go and get him for you."

Boggs heard more snorts, and then words whispered harshly. "What? What did you say? The Sheriff? What the hell's he doing here?"

Doug Forester came to the open door. He was of average height, complexion blotchy from years of drinking, eyes bloodshot. "What the hell are you doing here, Boggs?" he slurred. "Pretty damn early for a breakfast call, ain't it?"

"I need to speak to Walter," Boggs repeated what he figured Eunice already told him.

"Walter?" Doug Forester wiped his face more fully awake with his hands as if the name wasn't registering. "My Walter? What the hell has that boy done now?" His expression darkened.

As far as Boggs knew, Walter was a pretty good kid. Fair student, member of the wrestling team. Of course, Boggs was not aware of the day-to-day incidents at the police department. But Walter's name never passed his ear tied with trouble.

"No trouble, Doug. I want to ask him a few questions about Jake and Oliver. And I might need to take him with me for a bit. Jake and Oliver seem to be missing."

As he stood now, he could not look another person in the eye until he had a few drinks in him. And then, he became everybody's buddy unless they were law enforcement.

Doug Forester's gaze bounced back and forth and around as if trying to keep in focus, then zeroed in as he said, "You can take him for the next few years if you want. Save me a lot of wear and tear."

"Teenagers can be a lot to handle," Boggs agreed, hoping Eunice Forester would return quickly with Walter.

"What the hell do you know about raising a kid?" Doug Forester challenged. "You ain't even married."

The remark struck like a hard punch to the jar. Doug Forester was well aware of his wife's accident. But Boggs let the comment slide, seeing Eunice returning with Walter.

Doug Forester heard them, too. He jerked around. "What the Sam Hill have you got yourself into, boy?"

Walter glanced from his father to Boggs and then returned to his father. "Nothin'."

Boggs jumped in. "Walter hasn't done anything wrong. Like I told Eunice, Jake and Oliver haven't come back home." He directed his conversation to Walter. "I need you to take me to where you last saw them."

Walter's attention went to Boggs. His body slumped as if he were trying to shrink as small as possible. "It's got them."

"Who's got who, boy?" Forester shouted. "Speak up."

"It, Dad." His voice was small, and his eyes lowered. "Jake, Pitts, and I went to Eagles. There was an alien, and it..."

"Illegal? Damn illegals."

"Let the boy talk," Eunice coaxed.

Walter's eyes peeked at his mother. He took a step closer to Boggs. "You believe me now, don't you?"

Forester's hand whacked Walter on the back of the head. "Got yourself tied up with some illegals?"

"Here now, we don't need none of that," Boggs warned Forester.

"Let him talk, Doug," Eunice said.

Walter rubbed his head. He stepped even closer to Boggs. "Not illegals, Dad. An alien, like from another planet. Pitts, Jake, and I saw one last night. It chased us."

Forester did a double-take. His blurry eyes became more unfocused as his eyelashes fluttered with the effort of taking in what his son was saying.

"I don't think what you saw was from another planet," Boggs said to Walter. "But I am concerned. Can you take me where you guys were?'

Walter turned to Boggs. "I think so."

"What do you mean, think," Forester stood shooting daggers of contempt at his son. "You either can or you can't, boy."

Boggs told the Foresters. "I think it's important I go where the boys hiked to and make sure there weren't any accidents."

"If you did anything..." Forester began.

But the pressure of Eunice's hand on his shoulder stopped Doug Forester from completing his sentence. "That will be fine, Sheriff," she said. "Call us if you need us to pick him up later."

Forester quieted. Eunice Forester had more power over her husband than her petite stature suggested.

Boggs said, "We'll bring him back. I'm not sure how long this will take."

"However long you need," Eunice said. "I pray Jake and Oliver aren't harmed. I'll call the Pitts' house and let Matthew and Katherine know Walter is taking you to where they are."

"I've just talked to the Pitts, but I am sure they would appreciate a call." Boggs motioned to Walter. "Come on. We'd better get going."

CHAPTER SEVEN

"I shouldn't have come home," Walter said, sitting next to Boggs in the SUV as Boggs dove to Eagles.

His words matched Boggs' dread that he shouldn't have dismissed Walter's story as a prank. The boy had been scared by something, and that same thing may have kept the other boys from getting home.

Boggs bypassed the main entrance into the park that would take them down to the lake, and instead, he drove straight to the RV camping area where Walter told him they took the Summit Trail.

Cruisers with flashing lights greeted them. A white Command tent set and officers milled around it waiting for instruction.

Deputy Standwick came up as Boggs got out.

"We're ready to go, Sheriff. Where should we search first?"

"I'm going to let Walter take the lead," Boggs said, nodding his head over to the door as Walter got out.

Awakened campers stood in front of their campsites, wondering what the hell was going on so early in the morning.

Boggs told Standwick, "Have a couple of men begin taking statements. I want to know if anyone saw the boys coming or going. Ask them about other occurrences they thought were a bit off when hiking yesterday. For example, animals they weren't expecting to come across."

"We've already begun taking statements," Standwick said. "I'll add those to the questions."

"Good." Boggs nodded.

Boggs knew Standwick's childhood dream had been to play for the Kansas City Royals. He'd been picked first round, but before the first season started, a drunk driver t-boned his car, injuring his pitching arm. A dream ending before it had a real chance to take shape.

A team player, Boggs had never seen or heard him give anything but constructive comments to the other deputies. And competitive. Standwick, like Boggs, had an internal drive to follow the evidence to the very end, no matter the outcome.

Boggs added, "And call Park Manager Deputy Elizabeth Warner to notify her of the situation,"

"Done," Standwick reported. "She's on her way."

"I'm going to want Deputies Zehlke, Roth, Cory, and Dowling to come with me."

Standwick went to gather the men.

Boggs turned to Walter, who had come around to stand by him. "Are you ready to show us this burned cabin?"

Walter stared up at him. "Then you believe me now?"

"What I believe is that Oliver Pitts and Jake Cahill seem to be missing and that you may have been the last person to see them." Boggs knew he owed Walter an apology, but he was not ready yet to say the entire incident had not started as a hoax. It still could be a prank gone out of control.

Walter looked away.

Boggs asked again. "Can you show us?"

Walter nodded. "The place isn't easy to find, though. Only Jake knew how to get there, and he got lost." He glanced back to the entrance of the area. Boggs watched as Walter walked over and dropped down in the brush. He had rolled a bicycle out from the ditch by the time Boggs reached him. Boggs saw another one lying under foliage.

"See," Walter said. "Their bikes are still here. They'd have come back for their bikes."

The boy had a point, Boggs thought. The boys wouldn't have left their bikes to walk to the lake.

Boggs retrieved the other bike, and they took them over to Command. The deputies were waiting. Together they moved over to the trail: Summit Trail 2.5 miles.

With flashlights in hand and lit, they started up the trail in single file, Walter leading. They had been walking for about fifteen minutes when Walter stopped. He turned and whispered to Boggs, "This is where we thought something was following us. A bear. Or mountain lion, maybe. But then we spotted a bunch of deer right over there." He pointed his flashlight in the direction.

He had never heard of bears in the area. And a mountain lion was a real stretch.

The park was full of white-tailed deer.

Yet, nothing stirred. Not even a branch moved in a whiff of breeze.

They continued, and they came to a cross-trail in another twenty minutes or so. Boggs suggested they give it a minute. Sweat ran down his back. Looking up, he searched the dark clouds hoping it would not start raining again until much later in the day. Or not rain until after they determined what had gone on. And yet, he yearned for the rain to push back the blazing heat churning to make the day another furnace blast. To wring out the clouds and end the humidity.

Beads of sweat pimpled Walter's face, and his t-shirt stuck to his body. He signaled his flashlight to the left. He said, "You can take Bridle Trail if you want to go to the Summit." And then he shined it straight ahead. "If you stay on this trail, it ends at the lake."

Boggs studied the area ahead. Walter's beam captured a smaller trail moving into a thick tree line.

He took a long drink of water from the bottle supplied at Command. If the boys had decided to go to the lake and then were caught in the downpour before they got there, they might have camped out and thought to come back for their bikes later.

But how did they know their joke wouldn't backfire? Walter might not have returned to his house, considering his relationship with his father. Instead, he may have gone back to the Pitts' house. Woke up the Pitts and told them what happened.

Cahill and Pitts were not bad kids. And Oliver Pitts would not want to worry his parents.

It was not making sense.

This way," Walter said.

They continued a trail not as well maintained as the one coming up from the RV lot.

Boggs asked, "How did you know about this trail?"

Walter continued without looking back. "I didn't. I'd never been here before. Pitts, neither. Only Jake knew the way." He stopped short. Boggs nearly bumped into him. He glanced about before twisting to face Boggs. "I don't think we came this far. I think we need to go back."

"You're sure?"

"No." Walter shook his head. His eyes pleaded for Boggs to decide for him.

"We missed something," Boggs called to the others and motioned for Deputy Cory, last in line, to turn around and retrace their steps.

They backtracked.

Walter, now last in line, suddenly shouted, "Here."

Boggs and the others stopped. Walter flashed his light on what appeared to be a straggled of brush.

"Are you sure?" Boggs could not see a trail of any kind.

Walter shoved the brush apart. A bit of a trodden pathway showed. He said softly. "This is the way."

Moving into a dense ground of trees and brush, it was not long before crushed grass lessened on the slight trail, offering dirt and footprints. Sneakers. The prints continued moving deeper into the dark shadows from the trees blocking light, the elevation heightening.

The shadowing did little to lessen the humidity. Instead, the brush and trees held it in like a glass of water swelting in the sun.

A throbbing pressure was beginning to swell behind Boggs' eyes. Suddenly, he smelled the faint scent of burned wood, like a campfire. And the brush next to him moved as if something traveled past him. He jumped and shined his light. Then came another smell. Boggs put the back of his hand up to his nose to block the scent. It wasn't unfamiliar, but it had been a long time since he'd come across it—the rot of death.

Walter stuttered, "Can you sm..mell it?" His flashlight pointed in all directions, then straight ahead onto the trail. "It's where we first saw it."

Boggs stepped close to him. "Don't worry. I'm right behind you." Then, he asked, "Are you sure you can do this, Walter? I can have one of the deputies take you back down now that we know which direction to go."

"I'm all right," Walter said, continuing to lead them.

The trees separated slightly, allowing for better light. Up ahead, Boggs saw the brush sprawled back from a small vacant patch. An artificial clearing or created by nature? He wasn't sure. It could be a cleared camping site. From hunters, maybe.

The smell of wood smoke was heavier.

"This where we saw Templeton," Walter said.

"You're sure it was Ted Templeton?" Boggs confirmed.

Walter hesitated. "Pitts said it could be an alien, but it looked like him. Smaller, maybe. About half as tall." He nodded to affirm his decision. "It looked exactly like him." He hesitated again. "Almost." He paused. "When he saw us, he screamed and began running." His voice wavered. The fear returned now that they were closer to what had gone on.

Within a few feet, Boggs saw a deer's form. Not a large deer, maybe a year or two old, stiffly stretched out on its side at the side of the path. The eye sockets were dark, empty, bloodied holes. Ears were missing. Its gut had been hacked open. Cracked white rib bones showed next to red raw meat and black dried blood. Grayed muscle and intestines stretched out across its rump. It was not fresh, but Boggs figured it had not been here long. No more than a day.

A small pile of grayish-blue entrails, small, thin, were piled neatly on the ground. Walter zeroed his light on them. "I told them we should go back home. Jake had told us about other animals he'd seen killed. Animals like this deer. And I thought if Templeton killed the deer, then he might also have killed Jake's mom and sister."

He said, "But Jake said he needed to find out. And I couldn't leave without them." His voice fainted on the last words.

Boggs wasn't sure if Walter was saying he was too afraid to go back by himself, or he thought the other two would make fun of him for being scared to go on.

He exclaimed to Boggs. "I ain't no coward."

"Of course, you're not," Boggs assured him. "You came back here, didn't you? That takes balls after what you'd been through."

Walter sighed with Boggs' words. His shoulders sagged. Either he was relieved, or he dreaded what was still ahead. He pointed, "Up this way. There's more deer."

Boggs and the others followed, passing a three-point buck laid out in the same way as they found the first deer. Then a doe and two small fawns, white dots barely distinguishable on their butchered bodies. Boggs figured it was a small herd taken by surprise...by what?

What would kill like this? Each had a small pile of intestines neatly piled next to the bodies, almost reverently. Ted Templeton?

"Looks like a damn battleground," Boggs heard Deputy Ivan Dowling comment. "Who the hell would do something like this?"

Walter stopped them. He said softly, to where Boggs needed to step closer to hear. "Through there." Walter aimed his light.

"What's through there?" There was nothing ahead except for a dead-end—a wall of trees and brush.

"It was squealing," Walter remembered. "Like a pig, maybe. And it ran through there."

Boggs was having trouble placing the squealing sounds. Could he mean something else? He'd been talking about Ted. Crying? Screaming? A wail of some sort? A squeal was a strange way of describing what he heard.

"We followed it. To the house. And...the girl." Again, Walter stammered the words, and this time Boggs saw his body tremble. This boy had gone through enough.

"I want you to stay here, Walter." Boggs lay his hand on Walter's shoulder. "I'll have one of the men stay with you until I look around."

Boggs didn't know what he was about to find, but he felt there was no need for the boy to go through it all again. He made as if to go around him.

"No, way," Walter said. "Not after coming clear back up here." He jostled ahead. "Jake! Pitts!" He broke into a run, diving into the brush, disappearing all except for his voice. "Templeton, you leave them alone."

Boggs unsnapped his gun. He waved for the rest to follow him and hurried to catch up to Walter.

Was Templeton still here?

Boggs stepped into a large clearing on the other side of the thick, tall scrub densely packed between low-hung trees.

Walter stood a few feet beyond. "Jake? Pitts? Where are you? I brought help."

Not more than a hundred feet away, a burned-out ruin stood. Half a stairway remained in an interior of blackened timber. Yellow-eyed windows with jagged, sharded glass stared vacantly.

The kid hadn't been lying.

"Ivan?" Boggs called back to Deputy Ivan Dowling.

The others had followed—their voices echoing the shock of the find. Dowling moved up. "You ever see anything like this, Sheriff?"

"I want you to stay here with Walter." Boggs summoned the other deputies. "The rest of you follow me." He said to Walter, "Don't you move. You stay right where you are."

CHAPTER EIGHT

Boggs moved toward the house, then stopped.

At first, he thought he saw another dead deer but immediately dispelled the idea as he took in a dead girl's silent profile. He warned his men, "Watch yourselves. This may be a crime scene." He glanced at the ground—mudded from the night's rain. Evidence possibly ruined.

He knelt beside her. Her head angled back from her opened gaping neck. The ground beneath her blackened with blood. Her stomach area ripped apart.

She lay not more than five feet away from the house, but her hair appeared only slightly singed—her clothes, torn open but not overly scorched by the close fire.

Had she been pulled to this spot after the house burnt? He checked for markings that would show she'd been dragged. But if there had been any, they were eroded by the rain. She lay in a slightly sloped area that nestled her. Her arms were positioned comfortably by her side. Almost as if she had lain down to go to sleep.

Someone gave this body reverence after killing her, Boggs surmised. This was no animal.

Acid pulled up in his throat. His gut clenched.

This girl wasn't much older than the boys, he thought. Was she a friend of theirs? What the hell happened here?

"After we found her..." Walter startled Boggs.

Walter had moved stealthily beside him.

"Walter, go back," Boggs told him.

"We saw Chewbacca," Walter continued, his voice coming across drone-like. "He came from around the house." He pointed to some charred corner slabs. "Pitts was back over there." He indicated back to the trail they had come on.

Was Oliver Pitts the first who attempted to go for help? Boggs wondered.

"And then, Teddy. He was standing over there, behind Jake." He steered Boggs across the way. "Only, I'm not sure Jake saw him. He was kind of hidden."

Boggs was trying to map the scene out in his mind. Walter had said the dog came from around the house, Oliver east, and Jake to the south toward the lake. Why were the boys so far apart from one another?

He asked, "Where were you, Walter?"

Walter said, "Pitts dropped to the ground. It must have hit him on the head. Then he attacked Jake."

Again, Boggs focused on the distance. He'd said he saw Ted hiding behind Jake, but Pitts was the first to drop. Something wasn't adding up.

He asked, "Was there someone else here? More than just Teddy?"

"It was him. I'm sure of it."

Boggs noticed Walter's eyes were downcast. His brow furled. "It had to have been, Sheriff? Who else could it have been?" He wiped his eyes with his sleeve. "I ran," Walter said as if confessing a sin without the chance of absolution. "I ran, and I didn't look back."

Boggs twisted around and saw Dowling. "Take Walter to Command." He said to Walter, "If you hadn't come to my office to tell me, I would never have known any of this occurred. Don't worry. We will find Jake and Oliver. Now go with Deputy Dowling."

As soon as the Deputy and Walter were out of earshot, Boggs took out his radio. "Standwick. I need Dr. Potter up here immediately, along with the forensic team. No one is to come up Summit Trail. Call and tell Park Deputy Warner I am closing the entire park." Then, without a pause for questions, he continued, "Dowling and Walter are headed down. See that Walter gets home."

Deputy Zelkhe and Deputy Roth had already spread out, guns drawn, walking the premises. Deputy Cory came from the backside of the structure. "Hell, I don't think I've ever been up this far into the park."

"Well, someone has." Boggs's eyes rested on the dead girl.

"Jesus, Mary, and Joseph, poor kid." Cory crossed himself. "What do you think? A coyote, or bear, maybe?"

"You ever hear of bear in this area?" Boggs asked.

Deputy Cory shook his head. "But I never knew this place was here, either." He motioned to the burned house. "I'd say cabin, but this here looks fancier than a hunting or camping cabin."

Boggs got on his radio. "Standwick, I also need Chief Jenkins. We've got a structure fire." He listened. "No, it's not burning now, but there was a hell of fire not long ago."

He glanced around as he spoke and noticed how little of the structure's area was affected. What type of fire was hot enough to consume an entire structure without throwing live sparks? The whole section should have been ablaze with the season dry as it had been and with the only rain coming from the recent storms. But, instead, the area was cleared by about fifty feet away from the house-- a lawn of dried dirt. He surmised whoever had been up here had maintained the place from fire hazards.

Boggs and Deputy Cory joined the other two deputies walking the site. The last night's rain ruined recent evidence, but in a couple of areas where Walter had said he saw the dog, he thought he saw prints. And he found another set of footprints. Human. Shoeless. It was hard to get an exact measurement, but the images seemed much smaller than a fifteen-year-old boy's.

The girl's, perhaps?

Boggs retraced the trail where they entered. He reexamined the deer. This time with a keener eye. Each deer gutted. But, no blood on the ground. And no appearance of a struggle. The grass nearby was high enough in each area to have left some sign of the animal thrashing for survival, especially with the family group. Yet there seemed little disturbance.

Boggs was sure a poacher hadn't killed these animals. Boggs thought it would take a sick fuck to do this to an animal. He thought back to the girl. Her throat ravaged. Her stomach torn open. But she had not been gutted. Did that mean anything?

The whirl of helicopter blades sounded and led him back to the clearing. By the time he returned, an AirCare helicopter was landing. AirCare was situated at Pinkerton General, being the largest hospital in the county.

Dr. Cletus Potter, head of the Pinkerton General Hospital and medical examiner for the County of Circlegold, jumped out before the blades wholly quieted. Two others leaped out after him. All were wearing white overalls. Cletus Potter carried a black case.

Slightly past middle age, shoulders stooped, Dr. Potter came directly to Boggs. "I heard you found a body."

"Over here." Boggs led him immediately over to the burnt ruins and the dead girl. Potter stepped back as if having become off-balanced. He steadied himself by setting his case down. He shook his head. "What's a young girl doing up here? Do you think she started this fire?"

"I haven't got that far, Cletus. Jenkins will handle that part of the investigation. But it's sure funny she wasn't damaged much by it." He said, "I'm going to need you to tell me if she died in this spot or she was placed here after the fire died down. And look how she's lying. Someone took the time to situate her in this position."

Potter knelt by the body and immediately busied himself. "I won't be able to evaluate until I get her back to the lab. See evidence of any animal?"

"Animal?" Boggs looked again at her gaping neck. "You think it was an animal attack?"

"What else could it have been?" Potter returned.

Boggs couldn't help but notice how Walter and Potter's answers were the same. Yeah, he asked himself. What else could it have been?

He said, "So far, I have Ted Templeton and a dog. Could either one have done this?"

Boggs watched as Potter gently picked up the girl's head in his gloved hands. Scrutinize her neck. Then he moved to examine the balance of her wrecked body.

"How about an approximated time of death?" Boggs asked.

Potter stood up. "Rigor is lessening," he said. "I won't be able to tell if she was dead before the animal tore into her until I have a chance to do a full examination." Potter began taking off his gloves. "If she was alive when the place caught on fire, I'll find evidence in her lungs. But I bet that the fire died down before she came upon it. As you said, no real burn damage on her. The time of death may be hard to determine because of the weather conditions. But from the rigor passing, congealed blood, I'd say she's been here for a few days."

"Before the storm?" Boggs asked.

"Before the storm or right about then, I'd guess." Potter picked up his case. "As I said, I'll know more after I'm able to do a better examination."

He flagged his people waiting for his signal. They would ready the body for transport.

"Come look at what else we found," Boggs said. He led Potter out onto the trail.

"Whatever killed these deer may also have killed the girl," Potter acknowledged.

"What about the pile of entrails? Ever see an animal do that?" Boggs asked.

Potter shifted uncomfortably. "No. But I've been alive over fifty years, and I am still seeing things I never thought I would. And, I have to do stuff I thought only others could do." Then, he was startled as if his words were on a minute delay and he'd just heard what he'd said. "Well, best get at it."

"When can you do the autopsy? I need an ID as soon as you can get it."

"You're not sure she's from around here?" Potter asked.

Boggs shook his head. "Walter Forester didn't recognize her."

"Walter Forester? What does he have to do with this?"

"He and the two missing boys found her."

Potter returned no comment. Boggs informed Potter of Walter's story on the way back to the helicopter. He ended by saying, "Walter said the boys saw you at the hospital last night. Do you recall what time that was?"

Potter gave Boggs a surprised stare. "Me?" Then recovered. He nodded. "That's right. Young Cahill was looking for his father and thought he was in the hospital. I was attending a burned victim when the boy came into the patient's room." Potter quickly added, "Vehicle fire."

"Tornado related?" Boggs asked.

"An oil truck got the wrong end of the tornado's tail out on the interstate."

State Patrol handled the Interstate. Any other time, he might have heard about the wreckage and the injured, but with so much carnage from the storm, he'd kept his head down and handled priorities as they came to him.

"The Cahill boy got it into his head that the burned victim was his father." But, Potter went on, "I assured him it wasn't."

"Did the guy pull through?" Boggs asked.

Potter shook his head. "We did what we could for him, but it was beyond what we had to treat him. I had MedVac transfer him to the UI Burn Unit last night."

MedVac was a larger emergency air contingent and had helicopters close to the more extensive medical facilities in Des Moines, Davenport, and Iowa City.

"I received word he died on arrival." He added, "It was a blessing. He had third-degree burns on seventy-five percent of his body."

"Why last night?" Boggs questioned. He wondered why Potter waited so long to transfer him. As far as he was aware, Pinkerton General couldn't handle critically medical severe emergencies.

"I couldn't transport him until we got him stabilized." Potter redirected the conversation. "I'll schedule the autopsy for tomorrow."

"Still hours in the day," Boggs stated. "I'd like an ID today if possible and the cause of death. I can wait on the labs."

Potter glanced over toward the waiting copter and stepped in its direction.

Boggs asked, "Did you know this place was up here?"

Potter turned to him and grinned, "Even in my younger days, I didn't get much beyond Bridle Trail."

But Boggs wasn't in the mood for the good-ol'-days.

When Boggs made no reply, Potter added. "It must have been someone's hunting cabin before the state took over the park. Looks older. Clearly, whoever used it last wasn't being careful."

The girl's body and his team were already on board the helicopter. Boggs watched as Potter bent low and moved under the copter's blades as the pilot fired the engine.

Boggs' phone rang. "Hang on a minute." He removed himself from the noise.

It was Standwick. "We have someone down here at Command. The guy's asking for Bill Cahill."

CHAPTER NINE

At the Bridle and Summit Trail intersection, Boggs stopped. He longed for a cool whiff of air.

Suddenly, he had an overwhelming sensation of being watched. He heard the scrape of branches. The hairs on the back of his neck raised. Something shadowing him?

Just got the jumps, he reasoned. No sleep does that. Plus, he hadn't eaten a decent meal for a couple of days. A man cannot live on a burger in a box. Besides, anyone would have the jumps after coming onto a scene like he just did.

Circlegold County averaged five suspicious deaths a year. Eighty percent turned out to be the avenging anger from a spouse or relative. Not what he'd just witnessed.

He continued to Command, keeping his hearing acute. Each step followed by a studied glance around. All unwarranted.

By the time he got to Command, he was a dripping faucet. Yesterday's idea of things looking brighter in the morning was long gone with the day he had in front of him. Gray, gloomy clouds still covered the sky. The day set for sweltering.

Boggs took an inventory of the vehicles replacing the RVs and campers. A paramedic van was parked by a fire engine. The hospital's ambulance parked close to it. A crew crowded around a county tech van.

His hand went to his forehead, slick with sweat. He rubbed the pressure behind his eyes, ballooning into a beat of promised pain. Not bad yet, he grimaced. But he would have a hell of a headache if he didn't get some cool air. So as soon as he got updated, he was taking five.

Boggs saw Standwick come from around the tech van. He was also massaging his temples. The deputy caught Boggs' eye. Boggs gave him a curt nod and met him halfway across the lot.

"Did Chief Jenkins get there before you left?" Standwick asked. "State emergency service aircraft are taking him. The Forensics' lab has arrived and should be leaving in a few minutes."

"I didn't hear a helicopter," Boggs said.

"He may be coming up from the other side," Standwick said. "I was told he was leaving in five minutes, and that was fifteen minutes ago." Then, Standwick asked, "Any sign of the two boys?"

Boggs shook his head. "Did Walter get home?"

Standwick pointed Boggs over to the tented Command with a nod of his head. Boggs saw Walter sitting on the ground near its entrance. He also saw someone squatting next to him, someone he didn't recognize. Their heads together, the two were talking. Walter animated.

"I tried to get the kid to go home, but he wasn't hearing it," Standwick said.

Boggs veered slightly away from going directly to Command and moved to Dwight Sullivan, the lead evidence technician. From the corner of his eye, he kept observing Walter and the stranger. Boggs didn't like it. Standwick should have broken up the conversation. Walter shouldn't be talking to anyone.

Who was this guy, and how did he find Walter? Or did Walter know him? Standwick said the guy asked for Bill Cahill. Was this someone Walter met before over at the Cahill house?

"What can I expect when I get up there?" Sullivan interrupted Boggs' thoughts.

Boggs gave him his full attention. He needed to let Sullivan know that what he would find was no picnic in the park.

Sullivan and his team were responsible for securing all physical evidence. They would photograph the crime scene before making their inventory. Chief Jenkins would also call in his forensics team if he suspected foul play. But lightning was more than likely the spark that caused the fire.

"It's a hell of a mess." Boggs relayed the challenge of the location. "Lightning must have hit the roof, and an old, shingled place like it flared like a match to a wick." He told him about the body and where they could find the prints he had discovered.

"Cory is containing the site," Boggs told him. "Potter's taken charge of the body."

"Hell of a day for a hike," Sullivan complained. A backpack wrenched his shoulders heavy with what he would need. A video camera strapped to the backpack swung as he eased from one foot to the next, trying to ward off the heat with movement.

"The hike is the least of it." Boggs glanced up at the sky. "The rain ruined the site. And these clouds look like they want to take another dump. I want the entire area checked before more evidence is ruined."

Sullivan frowned. "I know how to handle a crime scene, Sheriff."

"I don't doubt you do," Boggs said in a tone that offered no sarcasm.

Boggs took no disrespect from Sullivan's comment. He heard Sullivan's parents lost their home from the tornado.

"You're going to find some dead deer. I want photos of them as well. Be sure to bag anything you find suspicious. Include all the open area and at least a hundred feet beyond."

"A hundred? That could take all day."

Boggs glanced at the clouds. His tone, serious. "Call in more help if you need it. And if there is anything that warrants extending beyond that point, do it. Standwick will remain here and be in charge. I need to get back to my office."

Sullivan glanced toward the path he would be taking. "Dead deer? How many?"

"More than one. And someone has done a number to those animals."

"Someone?" Sullivan said. "I heard it was an animal attack."

"No animal that I can name. Relay to Standwick anything you find that might lead us to the boys." Boggs turned to Standwick. "If there is any information on the boys, I'm to be called immediately."

"The second after I hear it," Standwick said.

Boggs made as if to leave. Then asked Sullivan, "Got plenty of water with you?"

Sullivan nodded. "We're good."

Boggs asked. "How are your parents doing?"

"Like everyone else," Sullivan answered. "Still in shock seeing their entire lives gone."

"Sorry about having to take you away."

"It's my job, Sheriff. I'll do a thorough search."

"I know you will." Boggs watched Sullivan take off to meet up with the other tech team members. Then he and Standwick moved on to Command.

"That's the guy, right? Sitting by Walter?" Boggs asked.

Standwick nodded. "I tried to tell him the campground was closed to the public, but he insisted on staying." Standwick said, "He mentioned you."

"Me?"

Standwick said, "If he hadn't asked directly for you, I would have had him escorted out."

"You mean he asked to see whoever was in charge?" Boggs clarified.

"Nope. He said he needed to see Sheriff Boggs. That it was important."

They were almost upon Walter and the man. Walter looked up and saw Boggs. As Boggs broke from Standwick and came up to the two, the man broke off his conversation and stood.

Boggs immediately sized the man up: Five-ten, hazel eyes, brown hair, with a frank composure, yet wrinkles around his mouth and etched on his forehead showing he smiled a lot. He stood tall, but not as tall as Boggs, legs shoulder-width apart. A military history, Boggs thought. Although the guy was dressed casually--hiking shorts and a t-shirt.

The man spoke first. "Sheriff Boggs?"

Boggs looked at Walter. "Are you doing okay, Walter?"

"Yes, sir," Walter responded, jumping up. "Did you find Jake and Pitts?"

"Not yet, but I will. You can count on it." Boggs then turned to the man. "I heard you were looking for Bill Cahill."

"Air Force Major Noah Sears." The man offered his hand. "I am following up on a report Major William Cahill may be missing."

The title confirmed Boggs's impression. The title surprised him. Why would a major in the air force look for Jake Cahill's father? And why did he call Cahill a Major?

"What report?" Boggs said.

"I think it would be better to talk about why I am here when you have more time to give me." Sears glanced around. "And when we have some privacy."

"My deputy told you the area was closed. We have a situation here, Major," Boggs stated.

"I'm aware," Sears replied. "Our concerns may be similar. I heard Bill Cahill's son is also missing."

"If that were true, and I am not confirming, whatever that has to do with the Air Force has nothing to do with the situation here.

You have been directed to the wrong person. And as my deputy informed you, this park is now closed to the public."

The man didn't bat an eye. "I am aware of the situation. Walter told me what happened to him and his friends."

Boggs frowned. "Do you need transport back to your vehicle, or is it within walking distance?"

"We need to talk, Sherriff."

If this Major Sears didn't mean to sound like he was giving an order or threat, he missed his mark.

"Who told you to ask for me?" Boggs asked. "Chief Moore?" Boggs glanced around, half expecting to find Purvis Moore in the thick of it. Only, Standwick had no more tolerance for Chief Moore than he did. He would have mentioned him nosing around.

"There's my dad," Walter suddenly shouted, pointing across the way.

Boggs saw Doug Forester standing at the blockade to the lot's entrance.

"Go on, Walter. I'll need you to come into the station later on today to make an official statement. Get some rest and something to eat."

"Thanks for your help, Major Sears," Walter said, heading quickly toward his father.

The pulse behind Boggs's eyes deepened. "Help?" Boggs inquired of Sears.

"I promised him I'd help find his friends."

There were two things Boggs didn't like about this man. First, he pushed his way into a situation without invitation. And second, he was making promises to a young boy traumatized by what he had witnessed and the possibility that his friends were injured.

"You can call the station if you want to volunteer. Ask for Deputy Standwick or Park Manager Deputy Elizabeth Warren. They will be forming groups to start a search."

"If I am right, and I believe I have a good handle on what has taken place, my expertise goes beyond a public volunteer."

The man broke from his at-ease position and stared at Boggs as if daring him to refuse.

What had Walter told this guy? Boggs wondered.

Sears stated, "I don't know if I got all of it."

Boggs startled. Had he spoken his thought out loud?

Sears went on, "He told me what he saw up there when his friends went missing."

Boggs said, his voice firm enough for the guy to know he was being serious. "I suggest you contact Chief Moore of the Pinkerton Police. His office will be able to help you with a missing person's report."

Boggs saw Officer Standwick was on his way over to him. "Now, if you will excuse me. I need to get back to matters at hand."

"Of course," Sears acquiesced. "I'll speak with you later."

This time Boggs was unable to hide his annoyance. "Again, it's the city police you need to speak to."

Major Noah Sears said, just as firmly, "I was instructed to speak only to Sheriff Boggs."

"Instructed by who?" Boggs insisted.

"Bill Cahill."

CHAPTER TEN

By the time Boggs got to his office, the pressure behind his eyes had increased to a hard, bass drumbeat.

The air was full of electrical charge. The temperature crept to a hundred with an equal amount of mugginess. A storm was waiting to explode.

Deputy Leo Mespelt glanced up as Boggs entered the lobby through the front entrance. Holding fort over the station while everyone was busy at Command, Mespelt looked disgustedly cool and calm. His uniform appeared freshly pressed. His hair, what was left, combed over to conceal a shiny bald head.

"I heard we got a shit-storm at Eagles," Mespelt greeted him.

"That's putting it mildly," Boggs returned, heading through the gate in the counter to the back offices.

"What can I do to help?" Mespelt offered.

"You can call Doug Forester and tell him we need to have Walter come in and make an official statement."

Mespelt picked up the phone. "I'll have him come in."

"Later this afternoon will be soon enough," Boggs told him. "Let the boy get some rest, first. His story matched pretty much with what we found at Eagles."

"I heard some of it," Mespelt stated, the phone still in hand. "I heard a girl was found dead. What was she doing up there? Do we have an ID yet?"

Boggs shook his head. "Waiting for Potter."

"Nothing on the missing boys?"

Boggs knew Mespelt wanted to string together all the pieces of information he'd gathered from the chatter over the radio.

Boggs begged off from going over the details. "Anything I need to know from here?"

"No one's come or gone since I came on duty." Mespelt tilted his head toward the coffee pot. "I just put on a fresh pot. Get yourself a cup. Do you need me to get you something to eat? You look a bit puny."

Boggs slapped his belly hanging over his belt. The middle-aged bulge reminded him of his struggle when climbing the trail. He vowed to get more exercise. Eat better. However, the thought of a stack of pancakes from Sally's sounded good. He was starving. "I'll make a few phone calls and then go grab a bite."

Sitting behind his desk, he picked up the phone and first called the Pitts family.

"Did you find Oliver?" Matt Pitts asked immediately on hearing Boggs' voice.

Boggs thought he must have been sitting by the phone, willing for it to ring. "We haven't found Oliver or Jake. But we will."

"We heard there was a body," Matt said hesitantly.

The rumor mill was running at a fast pace. Boggs hoped it wasn't coming from his men. He asked, "Could someone else have been with the boys? A girlfriend, maybe?"

Boggs could hear him confer with someone next to him. Probably, Katherine.

Matt answered, "We don't think so. Or at least we haven't heard of anyone. But you know how boys are. At this age, they keep their private lives to themselves." There was a pause where no one spoke. Then Matt exclaimed, "Good God, what were those boys thinking?"

"I can't answer that, but we will have answers. And soon," Boggs reassured him. "Call me if you hear from Oliver or Jake."

"What did you find at Eagles?" Matt asked.

Maybe he was afraid to hang up the phone. Perhaps he thought if he disconnected, it would be like severing any possible link he had to Oliver and his means of finding his son.

He must be feeling helpless, Boggs thought. No way to control the situation. If it were my son, I would feel the same.

"I can't go into that at the moment," Boggs told him. "This has turned into an official investigation. But, as soon as I can," he paused, rephrased, "as soon as I have anything tangible answering your questions, you will be the first to know." He added, "And Matt, don't take rumors for a fact. It just gives you unwanted grief where there may be none."

"What can we do to help?" Matt asked.

"Standwick is putting together volunteers to begin a comprehensive search of the park. I'll have him give you a call when he has specific times and places."

"Why aren't we be doing that right now? What are you waiting for? I'll get some people together. We will..."

Boggs broke in. "I understand your wanting to get out there. Sitting at home feels like doing nothing. But how you can help me best right now is to let us do our job. I will have Standwick call you. You're welcome to be at Command when the search begins. Or join the search. I will need to speak to Katherine and you again. Later this afternoon, if possible."

"We will be here. I may join the search, but Katherine feels it's important one of us stay at the house. Just in case someone calls." He paused a beat. Exhaled, "Do you know what people are saying?"

He didn't wait for Boggs' response. "People are saying we need to talk to Doug Forester. We heard Walter said the boys were kidnapped to keep them quiet about what happened at Eagles. That Walter knows who kidnapped them."

Boggs frowned. One neighbor calling the next *Have you heard?*

"What aren't you telling us?" Matt's tone was rising on the anxiety meter. "We need answers. You can't just expect us to..."

"There's no value in what you are hearing." Boggs emphasized, "I will keep you informed." And he cautioned, "Walter Forester is still in shock. I was with him this morning, and I am expecting him here at the office this afternoon."

Boggs was intentionally not telling about Walter saying he saw Oliver possibly hurt. He also didn't mention Teddy Templeton. There was no reason to add to the rumors. As for Jake and Oliver, there was no evidence either was hurt. Not from what he'd seen. Maybe the tech team would change that, but he was not about to run an investigation on conjecture.

"The truth comes out in the end," his father always said. "Whether you want to hear it or not."

He ended his conversation with Matt by saying, "I'd tell you not to worry, but if it were my son, I'd be worried sick. I assure you and Katherine, we won't stop until we find those boys safe. And at this moment, I have no reason to believe they're not safe. I will call you again this afternoon. Hopefully, with good news."

"All right," Matt reluctantly agreed. "But I'll expect that call this afternoon. I want to know everything."

Boggs could not promise "everything," but he repeated, "You'll get a call."

Boggs stretched to ease his shoulder weight from encouraging a worried parent when he had nothing tangible to promise but hope. Before he did anything more, he decided he needed that cup of coffee. And maybe getting something to eat was not totally out of the equation. But not pancakes. He needed protein. It was not only going to be a long day, but he saw another all-nighter ahead. Even if they found the boys, and he could not allow himself to think the boys wouldn't be found, he also had a suspicious death investigation.

He left his office and was almost out to the lobby to tell Mespelt he would take his suggestion and go to Sally's when he heard someone come in through the front doors.

"Can I help you?" Mespelt asked.

The voice answered politely. "I'm here to see Sheriff Boggs."

"Your name?"

No name was given. Instead, the person said, "I understand you're busy, Sheriff, but as I told you, you're going to find I can be of assistance."

Boggs stepped in the view from around the corner. The man he had met at the RV camp, the one he found speaking with Walter, who introduced himself as Major Noah Sears, stood in the middle of the lobby looking at him square on. As if he had been aware that Boggs stood close enough to hear.

"This is not only about Bill Cahill missing," Sears continued to address Boggs. "As I understand the sequence of events, you had two suspicious deaths before the tornado hit." He added, "The Cahill house was the only house on its block unharmed." He continued with only a slight pause. "And Jake Cahill thought his mother and sister disappeared the night of the storm. Jake said they were taken by something mysterious."

Boggs stood dumbfounded. Why would Walter have mentioned Deputy Wilcox? And the other person Sears was referring to could only be Royce Martin, who died of a heart attack right before the storm hit.

Sears didn't wait for Boggs to acknowledge the events. "According to Walter," he continued, "Jake thought he found his dad at the hospital, and Bill told him where he could find his mother and sister. The boys went to find them. What they found instead were a burned house and a dead girl. And now, Jake and his friend," he paused, thought a moment, "I don't think it's his real name, but Walter called him Pitts. A nickname?" Again, he did not wait for confirmation. "Pitts and Jake, Bill Cahill's son, are missing. Walter thinks something killed them."

The story had escalated from what happened to them to kidnapping and now killed. Boggs glanced at Mespelt, who was moving his head from the guy standing in front of him to Boggs as if watching a ping pong game. His ears opened as wide as his eyes.

Sears brought his overview to a close. "Walter told me he saw something at the site. Something he claims is an...."

"Remind me again who you are?" Boggs interrupted. He did not need more rumors spreading. And if Mespelt heard what he thought Sears was about to say, Mespelt might not be able to keep it under his official hat.

"Major Noah Sears." Sears pulled out a small leather billfold and opened it.

What the hell? Boggs noted the Federal logo. Why were the Feds here? He also noticed Mespelt eyeing the Federal identification.

Boggs said to Sears, "You can have five minutes. Which is more time than I have to give you."

Sears glanced at his watch. "Let's say my time begins as soon as I sit down across from your desk." Then, without another word, Sears walked over to the opening in the lobby counter.

Boggs heard Mespelt buzz Sears through. He heard because Boggs didn't wait. Instead, he returned to his desk, took a seat, and let the Fed find his way.

"Is this just you looking for Cahill?" Boggs questioned as soon as Sears entered the office. He wanted the man to know he didn't appreciate the Feds nosing into his business, especially without notifying him of their presence beforehand. "Or are you on assignment?"

Sears took the vacant chair across from Boggs's desk without waiting for it to be offered.

Boggs planned to let Sears stand. Put him on the defensive, as Boggs felt put on the spot when called out into his own lobby. Pushed into a meeting, he did not facilitate.

And how did this agent arrive at the Eagles campground this morning? The timing was suspicious. Boggs himself didn't realize he would be searching until the early morning hours. And how had the man ferreted out the only eyewitness to the event so quickly?

Boggs did not believe in coincidences.

Sears looked pointedly at his watch. "Time begins now, I believe."

If it was aimed as a joke to break the tension, Boggs wasn't laughing. "Should I expect other agents to show up out of thin air?

Sears sat easy. Smiled. "Just me." He added, "For the moment."

Boggs didn't like the casualness of the answer nor the underlying threat of possibly more Feds showing up. He also did not like how the guy had been nosing around without registering with the local police. Moore sure as hell hadn't mentioned him. Purvis wouldn't be able to keep that to himself.

"What office did you say you're out of?" Boggs asked. "I thought you said you were an Air Force Major."

"I was. I mean, I am. It's complicated. I am attached to a special division of NASA out of the Federal Office in D.C." Sears smiled. "I assure you, Sheriff Boggs, finding Bill Cahill is of the utmost importance. I am here to locate him as quickly as possible." He steadied his gaze on Boggs. "Unless there is a problem. Is there a problem?"

Boggs watched as Sears leaned back easy-like in his chair. He was not usually the type to jump to judgment, but he couldn't help but take Sears'question as a threat. The guy said if Boggs did not give him room to do what he came here to do, he would bring the heat down from the chain of command.

Boggs leaned back in his chair. He was not about to let this guy push his buttons. And, he was not going to answer a bunch of calls from higher-ups kissing the rings of those higher up from them. While political careers and positions of power survived by keeping the influence chain moving, he had his early-retirement date in mind, and it wasn't that far away.

Boggs said, "Per Protocol, I would have expected you to report in with either Chief Moore or myself when you came into town."

"Let's just say, for right now, I am on a few days of vacation. If there isn't a reason to bring about an official investigation, I see no cause to create paperwork for either one of us. I assure you I can handle my investigation without your assistance. I will find Bill Cahill. And you will find my help valuable."

He let that sit between them. Then he said, "You need to find two boys. I will help you find them before they get hurt."

Boggs didn't like threats. As if he knew more about what was going on than Boggs did. Boggs returned, "I expect to hear they're back home any minute, now."

The typical response would have been for Sears to agree that the boys might show up on their own. But Sear's eyes darkened, the hazel changing to a dull, gold color.

"I need to work with you, not your Chief Moore. Therefore, I insist we keep my presence on a confidential level."

The balls on this guy. "I'll need to have more than your word for that." He exaggeratedly raised his arm and pointedly glanced at his watch. "Times about up. So, if you don't have anything else, I need to..."

"I can supply as many words from as many mouths as you require," Sears replied. "Only, I'm pretty sure you don't want the Federal Government involved in your business." Sears went on, "Words have a way of getting out to the press. I'm sure your Chief Moore would enjoy taking interviews. But I think the Chief's contribution would keep you from finding the boys as quickly as you need. . As you said, Sheriff Boggs, you do not have time. Neither do I."

Sears leaned forward. Clasped his hands. "So, shall we get down to business?" He tipped his arm slightly also to check the time. "I have two minutes left."

"Two minutes," Boggs agreed. Boggs resented giving him one minute, but if it meant getting rid of this guy so he could get back to matters at hand, two minutes would be worth it.

Sears said, "Major William Cahill is also part of a special forces division. His job assignment, like mine, has a high clearance level. So I'm afraid I cannot tell you much more other than it is of national security to have him found."

He said, "You're wondering what kind of balls I have to come into this town, into your office, and assert myself. Tell you that you need me. Well, understand, this is not where I hoped to be today. I don't like having to face these types of situations."

Situations? The word exploded in Boggs' mind. This guy talks in riddles. But he didn't get a chance to ask him exactly what type of situation he thought they had here. And why it would involve a division of NASA.

Sears said, "Don't assume what Walter told you is all fiction. At this point, we should both assume there is always a great amount of truth in what may sound like fiction." He opened his hands, offering a possibility. "Let's say for this story's sake that parts of what Walter told you are true. Let's work with the premise that Bill's wife and daughter were taken."

"Taken where? By whom?" Boggs interjected. "If you have information about what happened to those two boys and that poor girl who I found up at Eagles summit, I demand you to tell me."

Boggs leaned forward on his desk, his arms balancing his weight as he bent toward Sears. "If Jake's mom and sister are missing, and that has not been verified, someone most likely took them to a local hospital. Many injured in the tornado were transported to nearby hospitals because Pinkerton General could not handle all the injuries. If they were hurt badly, they might not yet be identified. Saying they were kidnapped is a stretch without any clear evidence. Here in my office, Agent Sears, we..."

"Noah will be fine."

"Agent Sears," Boggs repeated. "We work from facts. Jake Cahill is fifteen years old. Seeing his mother and sister injured by the tornado could have put him in shock." He paused, adding, "Hell, we're all still in shock." He sat back. "Now, I'll tell you. Do what you must but stay out of my way. And away from my investigation. As I see it, you have no jurisdiction. Go ahead. Start your search for Bill Cahill. He might have also been transported to a medical clinic if he had been injured. Leave the boys to me."

Sears said calmly, "In our last conversation, Bill mentioned a place called Eagle's Nest. Have you heard of it?"

Boggs found himself lying and unsure why. "Never heard of it."

Sears tilted his head, narrowing his eyes. As if he'd heard the lie. "I am not sure it is an exact place."

"Then, if not a location, what is it?" Boggs challenged.

"Let's say it may not be a place or an exact location, but a situation."

Situation? That suspicious word again. Boggs shifted in his chair. "Sounds like a load of crap. What's that supposed to mean?"

Sears shrugged. "Again, I can't say."

"Can't or won't?"

Boggs glanced at his watch. "Your five minutes are over." Then, he added, "I don't like working with someone who I'm supposed to include in on my investigation, but yet they can withhold information. You want to see me again, make an appointment. I'm busy."

Sears glanced at the phone. "Think carefully when answering this call, Sheriff."

Instantly, the phone rang.

Boggs stared at it. He glanced back at Sears. What kind of trick was this guy trying to pull over on him?

The interruption was Chief Moore. He first asked Boggs about the investigation at Eagles, and Boggs told him he was in a meeting and had nothing to report. After all, Boggs was sure Moore already knew every conversation and piece of evidence found that morning. He was also sure Purvis was calling him to note nothing was going on at Eagles that he didn't know.

Did he also know about the Fed sitting across from his desk? Nah, he didn't think Sears was showing his badge around town.

Moore said, "I heard you had a visitor this morning. Someone is asking about Bill Cahill."

"If you heard," Boggs challenged, "why are you calling and asking me?"

"Bill Cahill's missing is a city investigation. You should have directed the person over to me."

Boggs glanced at Sears. "Which is exactly what I told him." Boggs grinned. "He's in my office now, and I'm just about to escort him around to you." The grin broadened to include Sears. "I don't want him to get into the wrong office again."

Boggs hung up. He said flatly, "If Bill Cahill is missing, Chief Moore is in charge of the investigation." He stood.

Sears said, "I think your Chief Moore is going to have to wait."

The phone rang.

How was he doing that? Boggs reached over and picked up the call. He found Dr. Potter on the other end. "What do you have for me, Cletus?"

"I had an unexpected break in my schedule this morning, Roger. I suspected you'd rather have that autopsy done now rather than later."

"You're right on that," Boggs replied.

"I'll be starting in about fifteen minutes."

"I'll be there in a few," Boggs said.

"The autopsy," Sears said flatly. "I want to be present."

"Sorry. I can't let you do that."

Boggs ushered Sears to the lobby counter and led him to the door. Outside, he pointed over to the entrance of the Pinkerton Police Department.

Sears made no move to head in that direction.

"Look," Boggs told him. "You can call whoever you want. But get this straight. I do my own investigations. People speak more easily to people they know. And with two boys missing, my priority is to them, not Bill Cahill or you."

Boggs refused to say any more or let the guy get under his skin. Instead, he went over to his SUV, got in, and headed toward Pinkerton General Hospital. When he glanced in the rearview mirror, he saw Sears still standing where he'd left him.

Boggs entered the examination room, finding Potter had already started the autopsy. While the room's filter system removed the contagions and some of the odor, Boggs still had never become used to the blend of rancid meat with the sweetness of burnt cotton candy.

"Not much to work with," Potter said when Boggs entered the surgical room. "I am classifying her death as accidental."

Potter pushed away the microphone hanging from over the center of the body. Examinations were recorded. But Boggs had often seen Potter stop in the middle of an examination, remove the glove from his left hand, go over to a clean area on the table behind him where he kept a clipboard, and make notations he might want to refer to later.

This morning, Boggs noticed there was no clipboard on the table. And while an autopsy could take an hour or more, this one was a record...fifteen, twenty minutes?

"What can you tell me?" Boggs asked.

"Hispanic," Potter began. "I'd say anywhere from thirteen to sixteen. Her neck is broken." Potter went on to explain, "She probably fell in her hurry to get out of the house. If I remember correctly, where she fell, the ground was depressed. Possibly from an old septic tank."

Potter gave a significant pause, giving a final sweep of the girl's body with his eyes before turning to a metal table behind him and pulling off a white, flatly folded sheet. He said while covering her, "I don't know of any Hispanic families in Pinkerton. So her prints probably aren't in the database."

He removed his latex gloves and came around the examination table. "Not much else to say."

"What about the house fire?" Boggs asked.

Potter shook his head. "I'd say she got out before the fire got to her. The fall was what did her in. I don't see any reason to send samples to the state lab."

"What about the gouge in her neck? And her stomach? Boggs inquired.

"Animals. I'd say she's been dead for three-four days."

The surgery door swung open. Major Noah Sears entered.

Potter called out, "This area is for staff only."

Sears gave a nod to Boggs. Boggs didn't return the greeting.

Sears remarked. "Good. I arrived before you started." He said to neither in particular, "I had to ask for directions. It took me a little longer."

Potter turned to Boggs. When he got no reaction from Boggs other than Boggs' eyes staring straight at the intruder, he took his glance to Sears.

Sears said, "I believe Sheriff Boggs will assure you that I have the authority to be here."

Potter's face reddened with the rebuke. He again turned to Boggs with a look that screamed, Who the hell is this guy?

Boggs gritted his teeth, thinking: He has authority. But he said to Sears, "If there are any further surprises, I will need to call for that explicit authority."

If Boggs was expecting this to put Sears off, he did not get the reaction he might have expected. Instead, Sears merely affirmed, "As I said, Sheriff, I have no problem with you making that call."

Sears walked over to the exam table and pulled back the sheet. He leaned over the body. "To see is to look," he said. He slowly moved his scrutiny from her head to her feet. "To look is to observe." As he moved, he took in deep inhalations as if breathing her in. "And to observe is to see." He spoke to Potter, "I am going to guess you have seen what I do, Dr. Potter. A young girl of Hispanic culture, around twelve to sixteen years of age. This cut in her neck caused her death. It was done by a jagged knife, maybe a hunting knife. The type used to rip through a hide."

Boggs waited for Potter to correct him. Potter said nothing, and Boggs saw how his shoulders stiffened.

Sears, still leaning over the girl, tilted his head to Potter. "I am sure you also noticed the bruising here?" Sears pointed to her throat. "It's the profound cyanosis that concerns me."

"Yes, yes," Potter stammered. "I noticed the blue-gray color. But the girl was in the environment for several days. And she was lying next to a burning house. So the smoke in her lungs could have caused the coloring."

Sears went on. "I would estimate she has been dead at least four or five days. The coloring would only affect her lungs if she inhaled the smoke when she was alive and breathing in the contaminates. This girl was dead before the fire."

Potter shrugged his shoulders as if trying to lessen tension. He said, "Lab tests could confirm the schedule if the death were considered suspicious. However, I judge that she tripped and fell, probably from escaping the fire, and broke her neck. Death was instantaneous. The activity from animals caused injuries to her neck and stomach. Possibility a coyote. Prevalent in the area where she was found."

Sears gave him a long look. Then, the silence between the two men thickened.

Potter glanced at Boggs. Boggs wasn't sure how to respond. Dr. Potter had been the medical examiner for the county for a great many years. His judgment had never been challenged until now.

"This child was murdered," Sears stated.

Potter opened his mouth as if to say something. Then closed it.

Sears recovered the girl with the sheet. "I'm sure that when the examination is complete, Dr. Potter will come to the same conclusion." He glanced to Dr. Potter, who stood scowling at the girl as if blaming her for what was just said.

"You're sure?" Boggs asked Sears.

Potter cut in. "The cause of death will be written as I told you, Sheriff." He turned to Sears. "Unless you have a license as a medical authority, I suggest you leave this room immediately."

Sears said to Boggs. "That call you want to make would tell you my authority on the nature of this girl's death should be taken seriously. And I think, if the doctor will continue his thorough examination," Sears looked to Potter, "he will come to the same conclusions I have."

He continued, "Someone in town murdered this girl. I think we had better find out by who before we discover more deaths."

He walked away from the gurney. Then he turned back to Potter. "It is my sincere hope we will not have to meet under these circumstances again."

Sears exited the exam room.

Boggs said to Potter, "You'd better give this a closer look, Cletus. And get me the completed report as soon as it's done." Then, without waiting for a reply from Potter, he left.

He found Sears waiting outside the room.

Sears said, "I must visit the crime scene."

At first, Boggs was going to push off the request. Going back to Summit Trail in the afternoon's sweltering climate was the last thing he wanted to do. Besides, Standwick would have put together search teams by now. But what if Sears was right? What if Potter did a sloppy job just to get the autopsy off his schedule? He had been overworked since the tornado struck. They all had.

Damn it to hell, he thought. It's this damn weather. To Sears, he said, "Will you be free to go in an hour?"

"I'm free now," Sears returned.

Of course, Boggs thought. But he said, "Then let's go."

Outside the hospital, a rumble of sound moved from somewhere close overhead.

"I hope we make it before this storm breaks," Boggs said to Sears. "You might want to take some rain gear along."

Sears scrutinized the sky. "Only a growl," he stated. "Should we go separately or together?"

"Together," Boggs said.

He didn't want to let this guy out of his sight. And he didn't want him around Purvis Moore.

CHAPTER ELEVEN

The sky, dark and menacing, continued to growl warnings.

Each became a little heavier. A little thicker in its rumbling. The thumping, pulsing beat behind Boggs' eyes pummeled harder. This second trip was not exercise. It was torture.

When they came to the first small clearing, Boggs stopped. Not only to catch his breath but to point out the dead deer.

Sears moved to it, and as he had with the girl's body in the autopsy room, he studied it. Then smelled it.

Boggs tried not to respond, but what normal person wouldn't have their eyes bug out? So why did this guy need to smell dead things?

Boggs didn't get a chance to ask. Instead, Sears said, "The sweet meats are gone. Whoever killed this deer planned to eat it."

"What about its ears and eyes missing?" Boggs asked. "Was it going to eat those parts, too? Damn, if I know of an animal that kills and selects only certain parts to devour. Not if it's hungry."

Sears shrugged. "I don't think an animal made this killing. I see no animal tracks. And the piling of the intestinal organs looks almost reverent. What did your Dr. Potter say? A coyote?" Sears shook his head. He looked inside the carcass again. "The heart, liver, and kidney are missing. Those are classified sweetmeats. On all animals." He got up. "Even ours."

Sears asked, "Straight ahead?"

Boggs resented Sears' ease with both the climb and the weather. There appeared only a faint glistening of sweat on his forehead.

"Have there been any other animal mutilations in the area?" Sears asked, having taken the lead.

"You'll find more deer up ahead," Boggs replied. "All look like that one. Belly's gorged out. Some with ears and eyes missing. But all with their intestines neatly piled next to them as if someone was going to sack them up for take out."

"Were all the deer killed in the same time frame?" Sears asked.

"I don't know," Boggs answered. Then, thinking, why don't you give each a sniff and tell me? He had seen other investigations and other investigators, but he had never witnessed someone conducting themselves like some cadaver dog.

"How about anywhere else around this area? Any other animals found dead?"

Boggs answered without covering a bit of snarl in his tone. "This is a rural country. And we just had a tornado comb through. So I am sure if you went looking, you could find a handful of dead animals. But, like I said, nothing like this."

"Where does the main trail end if we keep going straight?" Sears asked.

"The lake," Boggs answered.

Sears stopped. Twisted around. "Do you think your missing boys might have gone that way instead of returning on the original trail?"

It was the same question Boggs wondered. "I checked by the lake earlier. No sign of them."

"And Walter?" Sears asked. "Which way did he go back?"

"The same way we come."

Sears said. "We should take the lake trail on our return."

It wasn't a suggestion. Not a demand, either. Sears said it more like a fact. Boggs silently agreed and wished he would have checked it out before returning to the station this morning.

Deputy Jose Benito stood at the edge of the clearing where the trees thinned to brush, and the brush pulled short to open space. "Sorry, this is off-limits," Benito's voice warned. Then he saw Boggs, "Sheriff."

Boggs went to his deputy. "Hey, Benito. We need to check over the scene again. Has anyone been here since forensics left?"

"No, sir."

"Good. We shouldn't be too long." He started to step ahead, then stopped. "Has someone brought you water and lunch?"

Deputy Benito shook his head. "I've only been on duty for a couple of hours. I'm all right." He looked to Sears and waited for Boggs to make introductions.

Another boom of thunder rolled as Boggs turned to Sears, and for a moment, a brief second, he thought he saw Sears' eyes spark.

Boggs swiped the sweat from his eyes. Looked again. This damn weather, he muttered.

The ground area was pimpled with numbered, yellow markers from the forensics team. Pieces of orange plastic tape waved in the breeze on the burned building from the Fire Chief's team.

"Nicely maintained," Sears said.

"What?"

"The house. All of the vegetation has been kept away from the structure."

"Anyone with a cabin up here would keep the brush back in case of a forest fire," Boggs told him.

"Which means the place wasn't abandoned," Sears stated.

Sears gave Deputy Benito a nod of acknowledgment before heading to the burned building. He stood for several minutes studying what was left of the structure before turning to look toward Boggs and the deputy. Then he continued turning in a circle, his eyes checking the cleared, unvegetated land.

Boggs watched, half expecting Sears to sniff the wood as he had the carcass of the deer and the body of the girl.

Sears merely laid a hand to a burnt timber. "I may be off in my estimate of the girl's death," Sears called over. "This structure burned less than five days ago. I would say two or three."

Potter will like hearing that, Boggs thought. But he had a feeling Sears' judgment of how the girl died wasn't a mistake. And Potter still needed to answer for that.

He walked over. "We found the girl over this way." He led Sears to the side. Boggs could see how the girl had laid in a slight indention with the body gone. More blood than he'd first noticed had seeped beneath her into the ground.

"How far out did you ask your forensics team to go?" Sears asked, looking to the edges of the area.

"A hundred feet," Boggs replied.

"That should do it," Sears agreed. Then he asked, "Did they find anything disturbing?"

Boggs pressed his fingers to his temple. "More disturbing than deer gutted along the trail? More disturbing than a young girl found dead at a burned building, which I didn't even know existed until today?" Boggs itched for a cigarette, but he refrained, thinking it might be better to save his lungs for the trip down.

"Maybe disturbing is the wrong word," Sears offered. "Unusual?"

This word didn't exactly strike out the use of the other. "I don't have anything more unusual things than those I've mentioned." But, he added, "We did find faint prints from a dog or maybe coyote."

"I would like to take a look," Sears said.

Boggs led him to the area where they'd found the prints. Sears squatted. "This is too heavy for a coyote. Even a large one is pretty light on its feet." He got up and walked several feet in different directions of the prints. "No spore that I see." He looked over to Boggs, asked, "Didn't Walter say something about a dog?"

"Jake's dog," Boggs acknowledged. But he wasn't about to agree that the prints could be from it. He said to Sears, "Over this way is another set of prints." Sears followed him. "At first, I thought these might be from one of the boys, but they're small. They must be the girl's."

Sears squatted and measured the most precise print with the size of his hand. "This is much smaller than the girl's foot. And there's no arch." He pointed this out to Boggs. "Whoever owns this print is flatfooted. And see how the toes are spread?"

Boggs lowered, too, and studied the print. He had to agree with Sears. It wasn't the girl's.

Sears said, "I'd say whoever owns these prints walks barefooted most of the time."

"Summer," Boggs said. "People toss off their shoes or wear flip-flops."

Sears gave a nod. "Your people will double-check to see if the paw prints could belong to Cahill's dog?"

"Of course," Boggs said shortly. "I'm waiting on their report. I should have it by the end of the day."

Sears looked out and around again. "What was this house used for?"

Boggs shifted over under the canopy of a small tree for a bit of relief. "As I said, I didn't know it existed until today. Elizabeth Warner, deputy park manager, will know. Deputy Standwick is coordinating with her. Fire Chief Jenkins will include the usage and ownership in his report. I suppose it was an old place from before the park went public. Old timber burns like a matchstick."

"That it did," Sears agreed. He walked over to the burned ruins. He picked up a piece of small wood. And he licked it.

Go ahead, Boggs grumped silently. Give it all a good lick. You're not going to find one thing Chief Jenkins didn't discover. Potter may have acted like a buffoon, Boggs thought, but Jenkins had OCD when it came to fires.

"Your chief is going to tell you this was arson," Sears said. He tossed the wood to the ground.

"If it was arson, Jenkins will know," Boggs confirmed. "My guess is that it was from one of these last storms that came through. Lit the sky like a Christmas tree."

Sears shook his head. "Most definitely accelerant. The rain dissipated the odor, but the truth is always in the wood. Your Chief Jenkins will confirm my analysis."

Thunder blasted. The clouds appeared lower, darker, ready to unload. "We better head down," Boggs warned.

But Sears began moving throughout what was left of the building. He kicked at charred wood and ash. Suddenly, he bent over and drilled his fingers down into the residue. Sears straightened, Boggs saw a pair of handcuffs swinging from his fingers.

"I think I can just make out the manufacturer." Sears squinted. "Pearless. Do you or the local police keep a register of the number and types of cuffs held in your department?"

How had Jenkin's missed those? Man, he was going to be pissed.

Sears smiled. "The difference between law enforcement is that some are more thorough than others." He saw Boggs' discomfort. "No offense, meant," he added.

Boggs couldn't deny Sear's comment hit a raw spot.

Another explosion. Boggs expected a flash of lightning and more than decided it was time to head back. He was not about to stay in the open and get struck by lightning. But the force of the blast didn't seem to affect Sears.

Cold son-of-a-bitch, Boggs decided. Or maybe Sear had done too many investigations and became taciturn to the norm.

Sears walked over to Boggs and handed him the pair of handcuffs. "I'll be interested in finding out more about those prints when your team is ready with their report."

Boggs suggested for Deputy Benito to follow them. "Storm coming," he told Benito. "That'll do more damage than anyone coming up here." He also made a mental note to contact Standwick. They may have to stop the search until the storm moved through.

When the three got to the main trail, Boggs took the lead as if to return by way of the lake as they had discussed. But Sears stopped him. "We won't need to go that way," Sears said. "It's my guess the boys are still up here somewhere."

"And how do you figure that?" Boggs asked sharply.

"Those prints were heavy in the mud. Someone was carrying something. Something bigger than it. My guess is that it was one of the boys."

CHAPTER TWELVE

Boggs decided to make some calls as soon as he got to the station. He was not going to let Sears throw him off-balance again.

He switched on the wipers when he came out of the park and turned on to Highway 99. By the time he took the exit into town, he had to rev them up higher.

Sears asked if this was typical weather for this time of year. He wondered if there had been other disturbing situations before or after the tornado hit.

Hell, Boggs thought, if he didn't get this guy out of his hair, and soon, something could really happen to those boys.

As he traveled Main Street, Boggs saw people hurrying to get out of the rain. They were coming from the side street in front of the Pinkerton Police Department.

Boggs, with Sears following, went over to see about all the activity. He immediately spotted Doug Forester standing on something, flinging his hands in the air, flaying them about as if trying to bat away irritating wet droplets. A black bag, what looked like a trash bag used for leaves, covered him. A black cap pushed hard and low on his head shouted in white letters: GONE FISHING. Walter stood at his feet.

"What the hell?" Boggs muttered. He slipped into the crowd, making his way around so he could hear what Forester was saying.

Many listening were regulars at the same establishments Forester frequented. Only a few had come prepared for bad weather wearing colored slickers. Doffing billboard caps advertising their deep-seated desires, favorite activities, or the team they cheered on while sitting in their recliners. Those without headwear used their hands to give themselves a sense of cover.

Many were urging Forester on:

"You got that right."

"That retard needs to be put away. I said that a long time ago."

Boggs cringed. He hated the word retard. He looked to see who said it.

"He's a creepy kid if you ask me."

"Wouldn't put this past him. In fact, I'd bet money on it."

"Let's go get him. Get this over with."

"Damn right. I need a beer."

Boggs inched closer.

Forester said, "My son Walter saw that Templeton boy kidnap his friends. Walter would be dead, too, if he hadn't come to get help."

Walter gazed up at his father. Rain streamed down his face.

"That kid's been killing animals all over town. Pigs. Cows. Deer. You know it. You've been hearing about them. Weren't no tornado. And I bet you've been wondering what's happened to your lost dogs." Forester paused for effect, then shouted, "Templeton."

"My old Freddie's been gone for a couple of days now," a guy standing next to Boggs said. "I thought it was the tornado that took him."

Boggs saw Chief Moore under the door's overhang leading to City Police. He saw several other officers on the sidelines. Then he spotted Office Hayworth wearing his yellow rain slicker, his head gawking up over the crowd as a farmer would raise his head on his neck to count his livestock.

Boggs threaded his way between people over to Moore. "What the hell is going on?" Boggs asked.

"Forester's been ranting for the last half hour," Moore said. "He brought a couple of guys with him, and more have come off their stools to find out what's happening." Moore steeled a look at Boggs. "Maybe I should ask you what the hell's going on? And where the hell is that guy asking about Cahill? I've heard he's a Fed. Why did he check in with you instead of me?"

"Hell if I know," Boggs answered. It was an honest answer. "What's Templeton got to do with any of this?"

Moore snapped back. "I want to know about that dead girl on Potter's table."

"Ask Potter," Boggs returned. He'd about had it with others giving him orders.

"Forester says Ted Templeton kidnapped those boys. Maybe he also had something to do with the dead girl."

Boggs ignored Moore and listened again to Forester.

"My Walter was there," Forester shouted. "He saw him. Ted Templeton is a murderer. He took kids from our community. And if we don't do something about it, more kids are going to come up missing."

"You'd better break this up, Purvis," Boggs said. It was his turn to start demanding things.

Forester jerked his head over to where Moore and Boggs stood. Pointed. "They aren't going to do anything until your kid comes up dead." He yelled, "It's up to us."

The crowd stirred. Feet shuffled in place as if anxious to move. Boggs noticed one guy slapping at his thigh as someone would slap at a horse's flank, giddy-up.

"Got to admit, the kid's stranger than hell," Moore said a little too loud for Boggs' liking.

Boggs decided either Moore was ignoring the movement in the crowd, the whispering now growing louder, or didn't care.

Moore said, "Psychotic, some might say."

"Who's Ted Templeton?"

Boggs jumped. He had forgotten about Sears, and he was surprised to find him standing next to him. The guy was a damn ninja.

Boggs was about to answer him when something Forester said took back his attention.

"The kid's not human," Forester was shouting. "You all know that. He doesn't look human. He doesn't act like any of the rest of us. There's something more than physically wrong with him." Forester circled his ear with his index finger.

Heads in the crowd nodded. Others vocally agreed.

Then suddenly, Forester shouted, "Come on. We know where he is. Let's go get'em."

The cry to move was heard throughout the crowd. "Get'em."

"Come on."

"Grab him before he gets mine."

"Killer."

"Murderer."

"Templeton."

A warning shot blasted, stopping anyone from taking Forester's charge. Many fell to the ground covering their heads. Others ran for cover.

Boggs found his hand on the butt of his revolver. The shot had caused him to react. Moore hadn't given him a warning of what he was about to do.

Moore moved off towards Doug Forester, who still stood where he was, not following his own call for action.

Boggs heard Moore say, "Put a lid on this, Doug. Don't start something you can't finish."

Boggs also saw Officer Hayworth had pulled his revolver and stood with it in his shaking hands.

"Don't you worry," Forester loudly challenged. "I'll finish it. You ain't doin' nothing."

"That's my business, not yours."

Boggs walked over closer in case Forester resisted, and any of those lying on the ground thought of getting up and giving their opinions.

"Go on now. Get." Moore waved his hands like he would to an irritating fly. He turned to those still on the ground and those off cowering. "All of you," he shouted. "Get home, get dry, and sober up. You're not going to bring those boys home by taking the law into your own hands. Let me handle this."

Forester still didn't move, but Officer Hayworth came to action, waving his gun. "You heard the man. Get." He made his way around those on the ground. "Go home where you belong. We'll handle this."

Forester got off the upended box he'd been standing on, grumbling, "You'd better get hold of that Templeton retard before he ends up dead."

"Are you threatening me, Doug?" Moore demanded.

"I'm just staying," Forester exclaimed. Then he looked around, "Hey, where's my kid?"

Boggs looked. Walter was nowhere to be seen.

"Probably home where he ought to be." Moore steadied a firm stance. "You, too, unless you want me to have Hayworth place you under arrest."

Officer Hayworth heard his name and hurried over to Moore. "Here I am, Chief."

Moore raised his hand, palm-out. Hayworth heeled.

"Arrest me for what?" Forester slurred. "Freedom of speech is my constitutional right."

"Drunk and disorderly. Creating a nuisance." Moore ticked each possibility off. "And if I get any wetter, I'll haul your ass in just to get out of this piss."

Forester returned, "Mark my words. That kid is dangerous. I always said so. Tira Templeton should have put him in a home a long time ago." He started to take off, paused, "My Walter says he's the one who took the other two. If you don't do anything, we will."

He walked off. Officer Hayworth trotted after him to make sure he did.

Still unfettered by the rain. Moore tipped his head toward the overhang where Boggs first saw him standing. Boggs met him there. "Guess I'm in this now that it's crawled into town with the likes of him," Moore said. "I can't have people going off half-cocked. You'd best fill me in on what happened out there at Eagles."

Boggs reasoned Moore wanted information he couldn't get from chit-chat.

When Boggs didn't respond, Moore grunted, and his lips puckered with a sour taste. "Seems to me you might need my help. Dead girl found where two boys were lost. Young girl and two teenage boys. That doesn't look too good, Roger. Maybe they set that house on fire. They were fooling around. You know, as boys can."

"Interesting theory," Boggs said. He noted Moore made no mention of the possibility the girl was murdered. Hadn't Potter told Moore? They were buddy-buddy, after all. He said to Moore, "What about Walter's story?"

"Walter inherited his brains from his father. Only his haven't been soaked in alcohol for a decade. Yet."

The last, the yet, was said with a surety as if Moore could see into the future and knew precisely how Walter would step into his father's shoes.

"If Forester's kid says it looked like Ted Templeton, there could be some truth in it," Moore continued. "I'm going to check it out."

Boggs turned to leave. "I'll let you know when and if I need assistance, Purvis."

Boggs left. He thought if he turned around, he would find steam rising out of Moore's head. Maybe find his hand on the butt of his gun.

He heard, "Where's that Fed that's with you? I want to see him. Now."

Again, Boggs had forgotten Sears. Out of sight, out of mind. He glanced around. The area was vacated. Forester, gone. Boggs figured Hayworth followed him to the nearest bar and stood guard, ready to inform Moore if Forester decided to start something again.

But no Sears.

Boggs returned to his office thinking Moore's cooperation in mingling jurisdictions for the sake of keeping the populace cool-headed was a step to checking out what there was in it for him. And, if Boggs knew Moore like he thought he did, a man hungry for power, he would never be satisfied until Sears introduced himself.

Thunder rolled across the sky and with it a wicked-fingered fork of flash lightning.

He yearned for the change in season. The coolness of changing colors, crisp breezes. Hell, three feet of snow is better than this muggy shit.

CHAPTER THIRTEEN: MAJOR SEARS

Major Noah Sears strolled into the crowd.

Some ducked their faces as he passed so as not to expose themselves. Others rubbed their necks to wipe off the wet or strengthen their bravo. A few tugged their caps down more firmly, maybe asking what the hell they were doing standing out in the pouring rain when there was a bar stool with their name on it and a cool one for their dry throats.

Most, however, ignored his intrusion and kept their focus on Forester. They were memorized as if listening to an evangelist offering the possibility of heaven for those who thought their chances of going to hell were a good bet. Pearly gates? Forgiveness? Salvation for a life brought down by a shot glass?

"I'll have another."

"One for the road."

"Please, God. Make it go away."

Sears weaved in and around, having no real destination. Finally, he heard Forester shout, "He's not human."

Fear, Sears thought. The most potent weapon to man. More powerful than a gun. He stood for a moment watching the onlookers licking their lips, Adams apples bobbing. He could hear them asking themselves if Forester was calling for them to act but unsure exactly what he wanted them to do.

Sears empathized how fear could rip through the gut, tear up the spine, setting off neurons in the brain to act. But, no, he redecided, not act. That wasn't the right word. React. To move on impulse without thinking it through. And this crowd, at least those paying attention, might be set off. And those who were only half watching? They could be easily triggered to run with the mob. Of course, they might ask themselves why later. But not during the moment.

One of Sears' most terrifying memories was during the bloody Tet Offensive. The only reaction then, the utmost thought on every mind, was survival. Of course, he'd been young—only twenty-one.

He stayed in the military and continued a career in the Air Force. As the years passed, as his battles traveled from Vietnam to Granada then on to Libya, he learned to suffer in his fear. Mask it from himself and his men

There was another time fresh in his memory when he couldn't deny the terror slicing through him. He'd wanted to run but found himself frozen to the spot. It was the night he and Bill Cahill noticed something strange in the sky. Something that should not logically have been there. Something that funneled a light down on them and wiped out time.

Sears moved away from the crowd and circled back to Boggs as Forester shouted out, "Get thee behind me, Satan. Isn't that what the good book says?"

"He's right," someone standing close by shouted, agreeing. "We need to do something."

Another voice raised in volume. "Forester may be right. My boy Ronnie is only eight. What if that pervert isn't found?"

A chant took up.

"Get'em. Get'em. Get'em."

Fear swelled.

Then, suddenly, a gunshot exploded.

The crowd hit the ground.

The entire area grew eerily silent.

Sears saw Boggs. Then, he saw Chief Moore, standing close over by Forester. The police chief was holding his gun high as if threatening another warning.

"All of you," Chief Moore shouted. "Get home. Sober up. You're not going to bring those boys home by taking the law into your own hands. Let me handle this."

"You heard the man," another police officer wearing a bright yellow rain-slicker yelled. His voice was shaky but determined. "Get." He said it as if scaring away a barking dog. "Go home where you belong. We'll handle this." He kicked at one of the guys. "Hurry up. Or I'll place you under arrest."

Sears noted the officer was holding his hand beneath his slicker, positioned at his holster. Ready for more action if it came to that. Although Sears guessed, he didn't look the type to use his gun. His voice offered a trembling command of uncertainty.

CHAPTER FOURTEEN: CHIEF MOORE

"Hayworth!"

Like a dog with an acute hearing ability, Officer Hayworth's head popped up on his neck, and he trotted over to Chief Moore.

"Hell of a thing, Chief," Hayworth panted. "But I think we've nipped it in the bud. Moore ordered, "I want you to keep an eye on him."

"Forester? He talks big, Chief, but he's not much on the doin' side."

"No, you fool," Moore spat. "Him." He jerked his head to where Boggs could be seen walking around to the County entrance.

"The Sheriff?"

"No, the lamppost he's standing next to," Moore snarled.

"Right, Chief. What do you want me to watch him do?" Hayworth asked.

Moore said, "And find that Fed."

Hayworth's face crumpled. He scratched his chin.

"Now get," Moore ordered.

Moore went back to his office, ignoring comments and questions thrown to him by officers hearing about but not in attendance at the ruckus. He picked up the telephone. It was answered on the first ring as if the person on the other side had been waiting.

"Did you do what I told you to?" Moore said briskly.

"The report's like you wanted," the person on the other end answered. "But, if any outside source follows it, someone will see the same thing he did. Even a novice examiner."

"Then make sure the body's not around for another examination."

"How?"

"Just do it." Moore's hand clenched the phone. He hated inept people, no matter how useful they could be.

"What about the other problems," the listener asked.

"I'll take care of Boggs and the Fed."

"They're not our only problem." While Moore's voice came across hard and sure, this voice was scared. "There's at least three of them out."

"Find them."

"How? Ask for the police for help? That's your job, not mine."

"Listen. I don't care how you find them. Just find them if they're still around. My guess is those girls all high-tailed it out of here as fast as they could."

"And Cahill?"

"Damn it," Moore gripped the phone as if it was the neck of the person he was speaking to. "I don't want to hear that name come out of your mouth. You got it?"

"No one's listening to this conversation," came the reply.

"I thought you said you took care of that problem."

"I did. But his kid knows."

"I'll take care of the kid." Moore slammed the phone back in its cradle.

CHAPTER FIFTEEN: JAKE CAHILL

"Get away from me."

"What have you done with my friends?"

The place smelled rank. What looked like pieces of meat hung from stone walls. Giant stalks of dried grass. A campfire burned in the corner of the room.

"DAAIDDDDDDDDIDIDIDAWOOOOO"

IT had been screaming the same thing over and over. Tilting its head as if waiting for Jake to respond. Its lidless eyes were non-blinking. Then it screamed out his name. Or what sounded like his name, *"JAKKKKEEEEEE."*

The sound was so shrill it sent shivers up Jake's back in single, elevating rows. Zinged his head. His eyes visualized spots of color, deep reds, blues, bright yellows. Gold.

He was hanging off the wall like one of the pieces of meat.

Oh, my god, he groaned. Was he its next dinner?

And what happened to Pits? What happened to his mother and sister?

Over in a pile of debris, he caught sight of what appeared to be Pitts and Diddleman's hooded shirts. His sister's sky-blue colored blouse.

IT squatted at the campfire holding a stick over the flame.

At that exact moment, IT stood on its small rubbery legs. Crooked its head to the left and the right before walking over to Jake and raising the stick toward Jake's mouth.

Disgusting. Rancid. Good god. What is that? Again, Jake groaned. Or who was that?

His mind brought up images of the dead deer—the dead girl at the house.

His stomach roiled. He wretched. Vomited. Adding a fresh new stink to the other atrocious odors.

IT stared, its thin line of a mouth turning slightly at the ends as if it found Jake's reaction funny.

Then, when Jake continued to ignore the offer, IT took away the stick and returned to the fire. Squatted. And began to eat.

Thunder boomed overhead. A muffled blast ricocheted off the walls.

Where was he? Jake tried to gather his wits. Somewhere underground?

The floor was hard-packed dirt and stone. The muffled sound of the large blast of thunder gave him the feeling that the entrance might not be close.

If he could get away. He struggled against his bindings. So tight, escape didn't seem possible.

He studied IT. Thin. Small. Its skin was dry, grayed. If it had an age, it didn't show. Not young. Not old. Its head was large for its shoulders. Its arms hung long past its waist. It reminded Jake of something, someone, but he didn't have a chance to think. IT came back. It was bringing the stick. Something new was on the end, hot and smoking.

Had the chef thought he preferred it well-done instead of medium-rare? Jake almost giggled, then sobered. Not a time for jokes.

IT lifted the stick and meat to Jake's mouth. Jake again turned his head, afraid he would be sick again.

He needed to figure out how he was going to get out. First, he needed to find Pitts and Diddleman if they were still alive. Could he hope his mother and sister were still alive, too?

Maybe this, this thing, had something to do with my father. The thought of his father lying on the hospital bed, possibly dying, brought fresh tears to his eyes. The structure they had found burned to the ground. His father burned almost beyond recognition. Was his father in the fire?

Then he realized, "You were there," Jake yelled. And when he got no response, "Can't you understand me?"

IT stared. Then it pushed the meat at him again. And again, Jake jerked his head away from the meal.

"I'm not hungry. Okay. Now listen. What have you done? Do you have my friend Pitts?"

IT lifted its free hand. Raised two long fingers and what may have be called a thumb. Fat. Round. More of a stub. It tapped its fingers onto the stub.

"Is that a yes?" Maybe it could understand him. "Where are the others? What did you do to them?"

IT's mouth opened. Jake shrunk, waiting for the impact. Then, pleading, "Please don't make that sound." He tried to communicate the same thought by shaking his head hard. "No."

IT shut its mouth.

Okay, Jake reasoned. A bit relieved. We're communicating. "Look, you've got to let me go. People will be looking for me. You could get arrested. I won't tell anyone. I promise."

The thin line of mouth opened again, and it steadied its large, black eyes on him. "Jakkkkkeee." This time the sound wasn't a high-pitched shrill—more low-base, like static from a recording when the battery is dying.

"How do you know my name?" Jake whispered, unnerved. "Untie me. I won't run. I promise."

SQUEAL!

Blues. White. Yellows. Colors popped into Jake's mind. Circles of black. And when it stopped squealing, the sound continued pinging the receptors in his brain like a pinball hitting its marks, *ping,* faster and faster, *ping,* pinks, purples, *ping, ping, ping,* yellow, then black, *ping,* black, black, black...then golden.

All the colors stopped.

A golden light flashed in his mind.

That's when Jake noticed the marks on the walls. He hadn't seen them until the light in his mind flashed. But they were as clear as day now. Or as distinct as a day underground could be.

He'd swear he'd seen those markings before. And then, the name Max Lamott whispered in his ear.

Max was an old guy that hung around at Ed's Hoof and Beer. He claimed to be Lakota and made his living as a taxidermist. Jake thought him a great storyteller, and when his dad would go into the bar and get them something to eat, Jake searched out Max.

The marks on the walls reminded him of the tattoos on Max Lamott's forehead. Jagged marks like strikes of lightning. Circles. Some circles circling circles. There was a large line with a half circle on top. Like a bowl placed upside down on a table.

Were these like the hieroglyphs on the walls of the pyramids? How did IT know about the Egyptian language? Or had it met Max Lamott?

Hardly, Jake thought. Max Lamott died a long time ago. He was said to have drowned in Eagles Lake. An empty bottle of Thunderbird and his baseball cap were found on the boat dock.

But, if this THING did know Max Lamott, then it was old. A lot older than him.

There was a noise. Jake stared in the direction of the sound. It sounded like someone walking. Could someone have found him?

When a face appeared out from the darkness, Jake thought his memories had conjured up a ghost.

Max?

CHAPTER SIXTEEN: SHERIFF BOGGS

"Got a handle on those cuffs, yet?" Boggs asked Deputy Mespelt as Mespelt came into his office carrying a handful of files.

"We have Smith-Wesson, same as the city. I've called a couple of suppliers, and I'm waiting to hear back." Mespelt asked, "Think Moore's going to keep that crowd from gathering back up again?" He didn't wait for an answer. "I say, people are just plain stupid. I heard Forester was claiming Ted Templeton had something to do with those missing boys." He brought his hand up and patted his strand of hair to make sure it was still neatly in place. "Just because someone's a retard doesn't mean they're criminal."

Boggs bristled. "I don't like that word, Leo. I'm surprised to hear a man like you using it?"

Mespelt gave a dumbfounded expression. "Sorry? I meant no offense."

"My little sister was bullied," Boggs replied. "She was what nice people called slow. And she may have been a little slow at some things. But, let me tell you, she was quick to help someone in need or knowing when someone was hurting and going over to hug them. She had the biggest heart of anyone I've ever met."

"Had?" Mespelt noted the past tense.

"She's passed," Boggs said it low and flat.

"Sorry, I didn't know."

Boggs wondered why he'd felt a need to tell Mesplet. He didn't share his personal life with his deputies. And usually, he'd let a remark like retard slip past. But it was the second time within a matter of minutes he'd heard the term, and with its hearing came the image of his sister.

Boggs let the topic drop and flipped through the folders.

He pulled out Potter's report, scanned it:

CAUSE OF DEATH: Victim died from a Vic cervical fracture due to blunt impact of the head. Postmortem tear at the neck caused by teeth puncturing the jugular vein and hitting the muscle at the back of the throat—suspect animal activity.

Was Potter wrong and Sears right? But why was he questioning Potter's findings? He'd only met Sears a couple of hours ago, and he'd worked with Potter for years. He'd valued Potter's opinion good enough to make past arrests.

"How old was she?" Mespelt was still standing next to him. "Your sister, I mean."

Boggs slipped the report back into its folder, then set the folders on his desk to read later. "Too young," was his answer.

Mespelt scratched his head. "I won't argue Ted's a bit peculiar. But what would he have to do with the boys missing?" He wiped the air as if cleaning that idea away. "The kid's a regular Einstein. Doesn't look to me like the killing type."

Boggs asked, "Has Walter made an official statement?"

Mespelt shook his head. "Not yet."

"I need you to call Doug Forester, or better yet, talk to Eunice. Tell her we need Walter to come down right away and record what happened in his own words." He added, "Sooner than later."

"Right away," Mespelt turned to leave.

Boggs stopped him, "We need to keep an eye on Forester. And send someone out to the Templeton place. Tell Tira to keep Ted in the house until this all calms down."

Before Mesplet left, Boggs wanted an update. "How's the search party going?"

"I spoke to Standwick not more than a half-hour ago," Mesplet answered. "Nothing yet. There are six teams, checking six different areas. They should find the boys if the weather holds."

"Let's hope to God we do," Boggs said. "In fact, I going to Command and check with Standwick. See what other help I can get him."

"I'll get Walter down here." Mespelt went to leave.

Boggs called, "Mespelt?"

Mespelt poked his head back inside the doorway, his face puzzled.

"Have you heard of any dead animals found around town?"

"You mean like dogs or cats?" Mespelt gave the question some thought. "Maybe, and birds. From the storm, I'm thinking."

"How about bigger ones. Deer?"

"I heard about a couple of cows found at Royce Martin's place." Mespelt thought on it. "But that was before the storm, I think."

"Cows?" Boggs confirmed. "Royce Martin?"

"Yep."

"Thanks." Boggs got up from his desk, moved around Mespelt, and headed out.

"Where are you going?"

"To find out what the hell is going on around here."

CHAPTER SEVENTEEN

The windshield wipers dry-swiped the windshield *rub'bbbdud rub'bbbdud* as the rain began to lessen.

Boggs switched the wipers off. But it was not more than a few seconds before drops accumulated to where he had to flip the wipers back on again.

As he drove, his thoughts returned to his sister. When his mother got home from work that day, she didn't find Laura in the kitchen. So she went looking for her. Laura liked setting the table, and if her mother was late, she would begin cooking. His mother worked at Hair for You Beauty Shop, and while she never worked too late-- she told him she considered taking care of her family her main job in life--his little sister had become a big help if a client wanted a special "do" that took a bit longer than scheduled. So on this day, his mother was later coming home than usual.

His mother found his sister in her bedroom. Laura had tied a scarf around her neck and hung herself from the rod in her closet.

Boggs could still hear his mother's screams.

He never told his mother Laura came into his room when she'd first come home. That he'd yelled for her to shut his door and keep out. He didn't want to be bothered by his little sister.

A long-held sob pulled deep in his throat with the memory.

A stupid teenager, wrapped up listening to Bob Dylan singing *Blowin' in the Wind.* A record he played once a day, sometimes twice or three times. Dylan's lyrics touched that part of him wishing for the freedom of adulthood and wanting to see somewhere beyond the small town where he lived.

Damn it to hell. He thumped his steering wheel in anger.

If his music hadn't been so loud, he might have heard Laura.

Had she been crying?

Did she scream out?

Yell for help when she struggled against the scarf choking off her breath?

If he hadn't been so damn self-centered and told her to come into his room and talk, things would have been different. She might be still alive, living her life as he had been given a chance to live his.

"Keep an eye on Laura," his father always said. "People can be meaner than hell when they don't think much of themselves, or someone's a little different than what they think is normal."

Boggs could hear his father now. How he spit out the word normal, *normmmal*. A hard emphasis on norm. And he could see his father, at Laura's funeral, glancing over at him as if he'd let him down. An unforgivable act.

Boggs choked back the sob.

It wasn't until after the funeral he learned a group of boys bullied Laura when she was walking home from school. He knew lots of kids said things behind her back, but these boys had made Laura their mission.

Hey Laurie, bet you can be a little fast if you want.

Laurie, I want it slow. Come on, give me a slowwwww one.

Why do retards have such big boobs?

Show us your boobs, Laura.

His father learned someone reported seeing them following his sister. Grabbing at her. They watched as the teenage boys, several years older than the twelve-year-old girl, taunted her.

And did nothing to stop them.

"Where were you, Roger?" His father had asked.

Mespelt called Forester and the crowd just plain stupid. But for Boggs, the person watching while those boys badgered a girl to a point she began running, crying for them to stop, was beyond ludicrous.

And what about me? Boggs riled against his own actions. His father's disappointment was like a knife through his heart. But his cutting guilt was what was killing him.

He caught his image in the review mirror. Stared hard, "Doing nothing, you knotted that scarf for her," he told his reflection. His eyes grimaced with the truth of the claim.

Having found each one of those boys, he made sure they would never forget Laura Boggs. But the act never purged his guilt.

CHAPTER EIGHTEEN

As he got closer to the Martin's, a scent assaulted his nasal cavities. The Martins raised hogs.

He pulled onto a small drive with a white clapboard house. A tin-roofed barn and shed stood off the main residence with open, small wooden hog pens.

It was still only spitting rain—a lull between storms.

He knocked at the front door. It was quiet. He glanced around for a car to check if someone was home. Seeing none, he was about to leave when he heard the soft shuffle of slippers across wooden flooring. The door opened. A woman with short salt-n-pepper hair, wearing what his mother would have termed a house dress, slippers on legs purple with varicose veins, poked her head out and eyed him with suspicion.

"Can I help you?"

"Sheriff Boggs," he introduced himself. "Mrs. Martin?"

"Yes." She continued to stare at him. "I'm Ethel Martin."

"Sorry to bother you. I know you recently lost your husband."

"Royce," she said. "My husband's name was Royce."

The day the call came in that Royce Martin was found dead, Boggs arrived at the Martin residence shortly after Dr. Potter. Potter was leaning over Royce, taking his pulse and checking his vitals. At first, Boggs thought the man was still alive. Although, he was as white as a ghost. Potter continued checking and rechecking, going over and over, from the pulse in his neck to listening to his heart.

"Heart attack?" Boggs asked. Boggs couldn't get over how pale Royce's face appeared. As if every drop of blood was drained out of him.

Dr. Potter nodded, getting up. "Myocardial rupture's, my guess. I will know for sure if I do an autopsy. But, with Royce's age and what I see here, I don't think I'll put him through that."

"I am sorry for your loss," Boss now said to Ethel Martin.

Her lips trembled slightly. "Would you like to come in, Sheriff?"

"If you have a minute," Boggs said.

She moved to give him room. "I have more minutes than I ever wanted to have."

Boggs followed her into a living room displaying the life of an older couple, children gone, activity lessened to a recliner and watching television. A hand-crocheted afghan lay over the back of the sofa. Several books were stacked on a stand, along with *Game and Fish* magazines. Boggs noticed male slippers still setting by the recliner as if waiting for feet to fill them.

"Would you like a cup of coffee?" She moved as if to go to the kitchen. "It won't take but a moment."

"No, thanks. I won't be staying long."

She came back, going over to the recliner. Boggs wondered if she'd come to sitting in the chair now, filling it so she wouldn't have to sit and see it empty. She began to lower herself, then reconsidered, and came over to sit at the other end of the sofa from him.

She worried her hands in her lap. Glanced over to the empty recliner and then back to Boggs. "Royce and I discussed traveling the night before his death," she said. "We always said we would travel and see some of these United States once we retired, but...," she shrugged. "There always seems to be time to do the things that you talk about." She paused. Took a breath to steady the trembling of her lips. "Royce was still raising hogs, you know. It's not easy to get someone to take over chores."

Boggs nodded.

"Do you want to hear about that day?" she asked.

He hadn't come with that intent, but she continued with her story, nevertheless.

"My mind plays it over and over again like a record stuck in a groove," she said. "Royce woke with a yearning to go fishing. I told him the weatherman was claiming a storm was coming our way and possible tornados, but he wouldn't listen." She paused, said, "One time, Royce was hit by lightning. He was out in the field seeing to one of the cows. It was raining, and I tried to warn him it was dangerous and that that old lame cow wasn't going to get any worse if he waited until the next day. But Royce was not one for letting things get on. If he had it in his mind to do something, there was no stopping him." She smiled faintly with the memory.

"Was he hurt?" Boggs asked. "By the lightning, I mean." Electric storms were part of living in this part of the country, but he had never met someone hit by one. He knew statistics showed someone was more likely to be struck by lightning than murdered.

She shook her head. Boggs noticed her hairline slip showing white hair beneath her wig. "No, thank the Lord. He was fine except for a tingling in his fingers whenever there was a change of weather."

She bit her lip. "I should have known something was wrong that day. He could be stubborn. But that morning, he was on a mission." She paused, said, "Royce was a mild-natured man. In all our sixty years, he never raised his voice to me. But that day, he wouldn't hear my worry. He said he was going fishing at Eagles, and I'd see him sometime after lunchtime."

Again, she paused. She glanced over to the empty recliner. "If I ..." She didn't finish. Tears filled her milky-blue eyes. She continued, her voice trembling, "He came back minutes after he left. He hadn't gotten much down the road. I heard him call my name, and I went out on the porch thinking he'd left without his favorite rigging. He stood out there on the porch, looking toward the road as if something had been following him. He looked scared. Then, he dropped down and died."

She squeezed her eyes closed as if blocking the image from her mind. When she opened them, she leaned toward Boggs and whispered, "That fast. Alive one minute...didn't even have a chance to say goodbye."

Boggs wanted to stop her. He hadn't intended to hear her recount this tragedy, and he could see the retelling was bringing it all back.

But she continued. "I called 911. Dalbert Day, our neighbor to the south, said he heard me yelling, and Helen, his wife, sent him right over. But, of course, I wasn't screaming for myself. I was trying to get Royce to open his eyes. I was hoping he'd had a minor attack, and he'd wake up and tell me I was silly for calling the ambulance and bothering everyone."

She said flatly, "He never liked to be a nuisance."

She said, "Dr. Potter came right away. He kept telling Royce to hang on. Like me, he must have thought Royce was going to make it."

Her voice lowered. "Or maybe he was trying to give me hope to hang on to." Her voice hardened. "But he shouldn't have. If Royce wasn't alive, he should have just said so right away if he didn't have a chance. You shouldn't offer someone a rope, watch them grab ahold of it, then pull it away before they get a really good grip." Her eyes came to Boggs. "I grabbed ahold of that hope like I was drowning and going down for the third time."

She scooted a bit toward Boggs. "I grabbed ahold of that rope Dr. Potter threw to me. But I knew the truth. I knew Royce wasn't going to open his eyes. I knew our end together had come. But the truth can be right in front of you, and you turn your head not wanting to see it. You'd give anything for it not to be true. Do you understand?"

"I do," Boggs said simply. Thinking of those who were gone from his own life.

She suddenly said. "I don't know why I am telling you all this. You were there that day, weren't you?"

"Yes, ma'am."

"Why'd you let me tell it all again?" She asked as if more curious than angry.

"I didn't mean to have you go back over a time that caused you so much pain," Boggs said. But he was glad she had. He couldn't recall her saying Royce was looking back as if something was following him.

She dabbed at her eyes with the end of a sleeve. "I woke up this morning thanking the good Lord for giving me another day to take on. But sometimes the good Lord asks too much."

Boggs reached over and placed his hand on her arm. Thin, fragile. "I am so sorry."

"Not your fault." She glanced off across the room. "No one I can blame."

Boggs gave her a chance to settle her emotions before he asked, "I was told a couple of your cows were found dead in the pasture during that same time period."

She brought him her full attention. Nodded. "We didn't find them until after the funeral. I wasn't handling the animals on a regular basis." Her voice softened. "Royce would be disappointed in me for that. But, to tell you the truth, I barely knew one day from the next. Dalbert found them. He was trying to do what he could along with taking care of his place."

"Did Dalbert take care of removing them?"

She thought about it. "I guess he did. He must have called Homer Duel to come to get them. Homer owns the slaughter-house off Highway 35. But you'd need to ask him. Or Dalbert."

Boggs nodded. Asked, "Do you mind if I take a walk out into the fields."

She flapped a hand. "I don't think there is anything to find. Nothing left. All the cattle are gone. Most of the hogs, too." She asked, "Why are you interested in the cows?"

Boggs stood. "We have had reports of other dead animals in the local area. It's more than likely a product of the storm, but I want to make sure we don't have disease spreading."

She agreed. "The farmers around here don't need no more bad luck."

The small barn held stacks of baled hay ready for winter, along with feed for the hogs. The hog pens showed signs of a large sounder of swine, but it was now almost empty. From there, he headed out to the pasture.

Finding nothing unusual, he left the Martin place, driving out on Highway 35 until he saw a large sign on top of a red roof, Duel's Yards.

He pulled into the lot, got out, and went straight to the office where the window offered the sign OPEN. Going in, he was greeted by a woman with her hair pulled back into a hard bun at the nape of her neck. She was dressed in jeans and a t-shirt announcing DUELS. Her fingers continued to dance across the computer keyboard until finished. Then she looked up, "Can I help you?'

"Sheriff Boggs," Boggs introduced himself. "I wonder if I could speak a moment with Mr. Duels."

"I'm Mrs. Duel. Can I be of help?"

The door behind her swung open, and a man appeared wiping his hands on a dirty rag. "I saw the Sheriff's car in the lot." Then he noticed and nodded to Boggs. "What can I do for you, Sheriff?"

"I've just come from Royce Martin's house," Boggs told them. "She said you might have removed some dead cows from her pasture."

"Ja. Two of'em. When was that Hildy? Maybe two days ago."

"About that," she agreed. "I could look it up on the computer if it's important. We log all the animals we take in, dead or alive."

Boggs held up a hand to let her know that wouldn't be necessary. "Can you tell me if you found anything curious?"

"Curious?" Homer Duel repeated.

"Different from the norm."

"Ja. There was something."

Boggs waited.

"Damn'est thing I ever come across. Hell, I've picked up dead cattle over the years, but these from the Royce place sure took the prize. Never seen anything like it."

Boggs asked. "Two, you said?"

"Three," Mrs. Duel corrected.

"What do you mean by nothing like it?"

"Hell," Duel answered. "their utters had been cut clean off, neat as could be. Blood drained without a drop found on the ground. And their dang tongues were gone."

"Devil worshippers," Mrs. Duel muttered.

"Ja," Duel nodded. "Although how they did all it without a drop of blood spillin' is beyond me."

Boggs hadn't noticed any signs of slaughter when he walked the field. "Have you picked up any other animals in similar conditions before or after the storm hit?"

Duel shook his head. "And I damn hope I don't. Gives me the willies."

Boggs noticed a slight shiver move across Mrs. Duel's shoulders, too. Duel told him he only picked up the animals. He hadn't incinerated. He'd taken the cows over to Riker's.

Boggs took back roads, thinking about what Homer Duel told him. He might have expected to hear him describe how the cows had been oddly gutted. But Homer mentioned no likeness to the deer on the Summit Trail.

What was Mrs. Duel's comment, *devil worshipers*?

CHAPTER NINETEEN

Big money came into farming, and not many abattoirs survived the changes.

In fact, Circlegold offered only two Boggs was aware of. Duel's now acted more as a pick up and delivery service. They took the animals to local slaughterhouses. The closest one being Riker's in Pinkerton.

The Riker's building offered two entrances. First, the animals entered on what some folks called the dirty side. Then, double doors opened, and a removable ramp allowed animals to be led into the killing room.

Boggs had visited Riker's a few years ago when Riker called complaining of a break-in. The office had been broken into, but according to Riker and his wife, they couldn't find anything missing. "It was like someone just wanted to take a look-see," Riker had said.

The entire area, as it did now when he opened the SUV's door and got out, smelled of the warm blood washed off into drains, and more than likely, although he knew Riker held to all regulations, still leaked into the water table.

Boggs went over to the door with the sign in the window, OFFICE. Claimed by those who visited as the clean side, the application of bleach still did not wash away the lasting smells of fear and death.

Marlon Riker lifted his head to see who had come in. His face, grizzled from lack of a shave, startled. He peered over reading glasses. "What brings you out?"

"How's business, Marlon?" Boggs didn't bother taking the available chair. He wasn't planning to stay long.

Riker removed and folded his glasses carefully before setting them aside. "I've been going over the accounts, and no matter how much I add and subtract, I'm still not making enough money to retire. Corp farms are the work of the devil."

By Corp farms, he meant those farms influenced or owned and operated by large corporations pushing small farmers and those dependent on them out of business. Like Walmart took over small retail stores and emptied smaller cities of viable business and employment, corporations were removing those who made their livings by working the land and animal husbandry.

Boggs understood progress. It was logical. People wanted more for cheaper and would travel an hour further to get it. But that didn't mean he didn't sympathize with those losing what had always provided for them. Some of the local farms were owned by the same families over generations. Riker's, itself, had been in business for over fifty years. Marlon inherited the business from his father.

"I heard you're not doing much slaughter anymore but auctions instead."

"Yep." Riker pushed back his account books. "I make more money talking others out of theirs than laying out mine." His fingers played with the glasses. "But I don' think you came 'round to ask me how I'm fairin'."

"Doing the best you can like the rest of us, I expect," Boggs said. "No, I stopped by to check on something. I've just come from over at the Martin place." Boggs clarified, "Royce Martin."

Riker wagged his head. "Damn shame what happened to Royce. I heard Ethel's gonna sell the store. Can't blame her. Too much to handle, an' Royce should've let it go before this."

Royce Martin owned a small sporting goods store in Pinkerton. Most farmers in the area worked outside their farms to make ends meet.

"Royce always said he was gonna die before he got to retire. Damn shame, but I'm probably not far behind him."

"Hold on," Boggs said. "There's not that many years between us."

Riker grinned wide, showing two missing teeth. "Got twenty years on you, I bet."

"Hell, I'd have lost the bet," Boggs said. Smiled. "Look, Marlon, I came by to ask about the cows you picked up at the Martin place."

"Hey-up. Duel transported those cows a few days ago."

"Any idea how they died?"

Riker rubbed the grey stubble on his chin. "I generally don't ask how. Just cut'em up and incinerate. But, let me tell you, now that you've asked, there's something fishy about what happened to them cows. Homer Duel thought so, too. I think maybe we have one of those cults around here. You know, devil worshipers."

Devil worshipers. He would hate for it to become a rumor and panic in the community. Boggs hadn't heard of any cults in his County. Of course, he'd seen articles on the front pages of tattlers when he was in the grocery store. But he wasn't one to put much value in sensational news.

Riker said, "They's everywhere in this day and age." Referring back to devil worshipers. "But they keep themselves on the down-low."

"Why do you think it was a cult?" Boggs asked.

"No blood."

"Go again?"

"The utters were cut off the poor beasts. Other parts, too. And that wasn't the darndest thing." He paused before adding, lowering his voice with the seriousness of what he was about to reveal, "Not a drop of blood."

CHAPTER TWENTY: MAJOR SEARS

After park security verified his clearance with Sheriff Boggs, Noah drove down to Eagles Lake.

He stood on the dock, acquainting himself with the geographic area. The lake was large and appeared ringed by tall trees moving down to the water's edge.

Where were those two boys?

He wondered at the coincidence of the Sheriff's deputy's suicide. But he knew better than to try to link connections with frayed facts. He needed to be sure.

He tried to get a fix on where the trail from the summit led to the lake. Noticing a rocky beach area where open space broke in the foliage, he headed there. As he got nearer, he heard Bill's voice, *Eagles Nest. Home.* Noah heard him in his mind and the urgency behind the words warned Noah something was wrong.

The ability to hear each other's thoughts, even from a distance, came about on a day Bill insisted they take a hike. At first, Noah declined. The sky looked like they were in for rain. But Bill insisted they wouldn't be gone long. And Noah, thinking back, thought Bill felt compelled to be somewhere at a precise time. So he continued urging Noah out with him, claiming he'd found something that would knock Noah's socks off.

Kennedy Space Center, early Spring 1972. Bill had told him about the Eagle's nest he'd found. It wasn't the first nest built in the area. The area was known for nesting before the development of the space center. But it was the first Bill said he'd come across.

By the time they reached the nest, thunder had throttled a growl, like a deep base motor revving for elevation. Noah saw the nest. It was empty, nesting season over. And in a few minutes, he knew they were both going to get soaked. He wanted to head back immediately.

Another deep booming sound, this time more like a plane breaking the sound barrier.

"That's interesting, Bill," Noah joshed him, "but did you bring me all this way, with a storm brewing, to see an eagle's nest built on top of an electric pole? Couldn't we have waited for a nicer day? Or maybe spring, during nesting season?"

Bill gave him a weird glance. "I could have sworn I was just here yesterday, and the nest was active."

"Kids grow up fast," Noah laughed. "Even the bird kind. But if we don't get back to the base, we're going to get drenched."

But Bill couldn't stop staring up at the nest, as if expecting the Eagles to fly back and prove him right.

Noah felt the first drops of rain. "Come on. We'll come back some other time. If they nest here, they'll be back."

Reluctantly, Bill turned to go. Only, they hadn't gone more than a few feet when the large bilious cloud above them parted. A gust of wind blew from it, and then came a brilliant light.

A helicopter searchlight? He shaded his eyes to get a better view. "What's coming at us, Bill?"

Noah saw Bill encircled by the light. Then the circle enlarged and took him into it.

"What is it?" Bill shouted.

Noah felt himself rising off the ground. He resisted, but his arms and legs refused to obey his frantic mental commands.

The next Noah knew, he woke in his apartment.

He found himself still in the clothes he'd worn hiking, and he was lying on top of the covers as if he'd come in too tired to pull back the sheets.

An alarm went off. The hands on the clock radio beside his bed showed six-thirty.

A dream? It was his first thought.

He sat up. Grabbed his head. He figured they must have gone out drinking after coming back. Rode out the storm with pizza and beer. But neither he nor Bill drank a lot. Not so much to bring them home drunk, fall into bed, and pass out.

A pain zinged the middle of his forehead, like the remnants of a brain freeze from chewing on ice. A sour tang smothered thick on his tongue, tasting medicinal.

He went to stand. But like when in space for an extended period without gravity, his joints and muscles ached. His legs folded under him.

He sat back down and took long deep breaths. He replayed what he could remember. Meeting Bill. Bill said he would knock his socks off on a hike to see the Eagle's nest. He regarded his feet. Socks were still on. Hell, he hadn't bothered removing his shoes. Then, something? He couldn't quite remember. What was it? Thunder? A light?

He forced himself to stand up. Why couldn't he remember? He called Bill.

Bill answered on the first ring. "Good thing you called. I could have slept a week."

"Do you know what time it is?" Noah asked him.

"Damn, six-thirty. I'm supposed to meet Colonel Sharp for dinner tonight."

"Look out the window, Bill. Morning's breaking outside."

He heard Bill's footsteps slap across the room. A window was thrown open. Then, a shout, "What the hell?" Hurried footsteps back.

Bill repeated the exclamation, "What the fuck?"

"That's putting it lightly," Noah returned. "Something happened to us on our hike. Do you remember anything?"

"Ah, no...no. I don't even remember coming back here."

"You still dressed like yesterday?"

"Yeah?" The answer told Noah that Bill's awareness was hazy. Like he was still half asleep.

"We need to get together. Figure out what we can remember," Noah said. He heard the worrying uncertainty in his voice. "Bill. We've somehow lost 16 hours."

They sat at Stoney's Café, drinking black coffee, trying to remove the cobwebs. They began by sharing what they could piece together. Some memory returned as the pieces fit.

"Like I was flying," Bill remembered. "I could see the entire space center."

Noah had a little memory of this, too.

"One hell of a dream," Bill said.

"We couldn't have had the same dream," Noah told him.

After that, each time they got together, they shared newer memories. Bill told Noah he had had strange dreams. Nightmares where he found himself lying on a gurney, and he felt like there was something else with him, but he couldn't see anything because the overhead light blinded him. But he could feel something touch him. Poke him. A couple of times, he was poked with something so sharp he thought he was being operated on without an anesthetic.

His nightmare equaled Noah's.

After Noah admitted to having the same type of nightmare, he pulled up his shirt to show Bill the marks on his body. "And not only on my chest. I have markings on my stomach and groin area."

Bill nodded. Showed his own marks.

They took their story to their command, to Colonel Sharp.

At first, Colonel Sharp dismissed their story, claiming they were trying to pull one over on him. That Bill fabled up an account to get out of missing their dinner.

As time continued, he and Bill realized they had developed telepathy since the experience. Sharing this discovery with Colonel Sharp, superiors treated them differently. The ESP had begun in a simple form. Noah knew what Bill was going to say before he said it. Maybe no different than a husband or wife, or two people who know each other. Only then Noah started hearing Bill's thoughts without being in the same room. Like a whisper in his ear. Or mind. Distance eventually was not a requirement for either of them.

They were tested and poked and probed, just like in their nightmare. Then, General Walter Musk from the Pentagon interviewed them separately. They were given lie-detector tests and analyzed by a psychiatrist. Asked if they would agree to be hypnotized.

He and Bill were not notified of what occurred during their separate hypnotic sessions but found themselves immediately transferred to a division in Washington, D. C. A special division of government noted as "Top Secret." Their names blackened out in files or entirely deleted.

They were introduced to others who no longer existed on government records. Bill once joked the president didn't even have clearance for this division. Their mission was to meet with those who claimed to have had the same type of experiences as he and

Bill, with what they now termed unidentified flying objects. They were sent to convince those people that what they saw wasn't real-- while confiscating any film footage or data accumulated.

Bill? Noah called in his mind, concentrating. *Where are you?*

No answer

And then he caught sight of someone coming out from where he estimated the path from the Summit emptied. This person was too tall to be one of the boys.

Bill?

CHAPTER TWENTY-ONE

The man glanced back as if trying to determine whether to be approached by Noah or return from where he had come.

He was lean and tall and walked with a slight catch in his step. His skin, darkened and dry, weathered, gave the appearance he spent a significant amount of time outside. A receding hairline broadened his forehead. And what was left of his coarse black hair, he'd tied in a long tail down his back.

He was wearing jeans, old and white-washed with wear, with a large rip on his left knee. The mud that obscured his sneakers' whiteness matched the splatter on his clothes.

This was not Bill.

The man took a long-steadied study of him. "You the cops?"

Noah shook his head. "Not a member of the local police," he said truthfully. "I'm looking for two boys. You haven't seen them, have you? Jake Cahill, Bill Cahill's son, and his friend Oliver Pitts."

"Haven't seen anyone but cops," the man responded.

His neck showed a tattoo of an eagle's body designed out of a squared hourglass, with lightning strikes overhead and two lines separated by black dots. His dirty plaid shirt, unbuttoned due to the heat, exposed another large, squared-hourglass eagle tattooed on his chest.

The man sucked the inside of his cheek. He turned his head and spit. "You're one of them, ain't you? I can tell by the eyes." He wiped away a spit of yellow from his lips.

"I told you, I'm not with the police. The boys have been missing since last night. In this weather, we must find them."

"Can't find what doesn't want to be found," the man said.

He reeked of cannabis.

"I don't understand," Noah said. "Then you have seen them?"

The man didn't answer. Noah tried again. "There is a house from the way you've come. It recently caught on fire. Do you know anything about it? Do you know Bill Cahill? He may have been in the fire."

The man twisted his face in disgust. "Sica."

"Sica?" Noah repeated, hearing the word pronounced *see-chah.* "I'm not familiar with the term."

"Evil." The man leaned toward Noah. His face darkened. "The end times are comin', brother. But not for us. We've got a 'ways to go. And not all of us are worthy of following."

"Where are we going?" Noah asked curiously.

"Home. Wankantanka." The man turned to leave.

Noah called out to stop him. "Look, if you know anything, if you have seen anything, we could use your help."

The man crossed his arms over his chest, steadied his legs shoulder-width apart. "I am Chatan, son of Max. I am Lakota."

To Bill, Chatan looked more northern European than American Indian. "Nice to meet you, Chatan. Look, again, if you see two boys, please let the local authorities know." Then, figuring the guy spent a good amount of time up in the woods, he might be aware of unmarked areas. Those places not generally public. "Have you heard about a place called Eagle's Nest here in the park? Do you know where that might be?"

"Eagles," the guy repeated. Smiled. "Wabli peta."

The smile offered Noah hope. He repeated, "Wahn-blee pay-dah." He said, "Sorry, you're speaking Greek to me. What does it mean?"

The smile turned into a frown. Chatan was not amused. "My father told me of the times before the end times. Then, like now, there were a great many cities. People lived full lives. They drank of the manta. Saw the pure spirit. But days became days. Cities grew together. The manta drunk dry by greedy mouths. People grew blind to pure spirit." He held up his hand and motioned to the clouds overhead. "The storms came. Eagles flew out of the black clouds full of fire. They took those who were not blind. They hunted and took what flew in the sky and what moved on land. The waters poured from the heavens." He paused. Grunted. "When the great storm ended, the waters receded. Mother earth again bore her children."

Noah knew the biblical flood story was not unique. Many cultures from many ages had the same type of myths.

"The end times are near again." Chatan continued, "The eagles are returning."

He did not pause. "Walbi Peta. Fire Eagles from the sky. Black Elk, our great Lakota, knew the voice of the creator. He was made of pure spirit." Chatan raised his index finger to the dark sky above. Then in one swift movement, he swung his hand down and poked his finger into the middle of Noah's forehead. "It is in the eyes. The truth cannot be hidden from those who know. The time is near. It is not time for you. But some you know will be leaving."

His move was so unexpected, his finger causing a jolt of surprise, that Noah jerked back and away.

Chatan turned his head and spat yellow juice out on the ground. He squinted one eye. "They killed my father. They will kill me."

"Who? The fire eagles?" Noah was having trouble untangling precisely who this man was talking about. And what were the eagles? Did it relate to Bill's *Eagles' Nest*?

"People don't like different even when we all came from same." Chatan stepped around Noah, ending the conversation.

Noah watched him move past the dock area, walk across to the parking lot, and proceed up the entrance road out of sight. He made a mental note to tell Boggs about the guy. Although Noah didn't think the man was a threat to anyone but himself.

If the guy...what did he call himself? Chatan? Son of Max? If he had seen two missing boys, would he have even mentioned them? If he knew the meaning or the location of Eagles' Nest, would he have said?

No, he decided. If Chatan thought the boys were in trouble, he was more the type to cover for them.

He thought again about how Chatan declared that he, Noah, was one of them.

CHAPTER TWENTY-TWO

Noah walked over to the area where Chatan appeared.

He found a faint trail. Not overly used. He figured most hikers familiar with the park would go up the Summit Trail, and at the junction, they would turn toward the summit area or turn in the opposite direction where Noah guessed the horse stables could be found. After all, the junction trail was called the Bridle Trail. Hikers would not necessarily know to keep going straight on a less-traveled route.

Taking a glance at the sky, he saw the storm held waiting. He moved from lake brush and small trees to a forest of white oaks. The trail was steep and called for sure-footedness. His fatigue and exertion thumped an ache in his head. He knew he needed to eat and promised he would as soon as he'd paid another visit to the crime scene. He wanted to observe it uninterrupted.

Walter's story played in his mind as he hiked. He understood why the events stymied Sheriff Boggs. If Noah hadn't had his own experience with the unexplainable, he would have been, too. But since he'd been working in special forces, he'd investigated numerous stories not unlike this one.

After the case of Betty and Barney Hill's story in the '60s of abduction, thousands of people started claiming that they, too, experienced a missing time episode. Noah learned that lost time was more like a gap in conscious memory. Images hidden deep in the psyche, wrapped by denial, or completely erased. Often memory could only be recovered through dreams or hypnosis.

Yet, maybe because there had been no loss of time, no void between conscious moments, Walter's accounting came across as an accurate recollection.

Arriving at the crime scene, he went directly to the burned structure, where he found the handcuffs. Found, he knew, was not the accurate verb. Most think of found as an effect from the act of chance or unexpected discovery. However, since that day when his life changed, he opened himself to being led.

Telepathy had been the first significant change. Then, more of his senses developed extrasensory. His brain triggered the slightest scent. Like a dog has an olfactory of more than three hundred million receptors to a human's six million, Noah could sniff out the slightest scent present or not fully dissipated. A common fish, the catfish, maybe even those caught here in Eagles Lake, has the most fantastic sense of taste. Having one hundred seventy-five sensors, compared to a human's ten thousand. But Noah's mouth and skin perceived the slightest modicum of taste. And hearing? A simple moth. Well, maybe not so simple. After it, the bat, owl, elephant, and Noah's hearing, surpassed any other human's that Noah knew. Expect for others likewise affected in special forces.

He stood in the center of the ash and ruin of the building. What caused these changes in him? And in Bill? And in the others, they had met while in the special forces unit? He still had only questions, the answers within possible reach but held at a distance.

He laid his hand on a piece of charred wood. He struggled as the vibrations moved through him, giving off the energy of the inferno that blackened the edifice. Severe. Intense and quick. He again put his tongue to the wood. There was no doubt. When Noah's tongue lifted off the wood, his brain registered a liquid sharply pungent, oily. He tasted and smelled Benzene. Strong. Saturated.

He moved from the burned structure to where the body had lain. He stared at the impression in the ground. He was hesitant. He knew what to expect, but that didn't make what he was about to do any easier.

He squatted and placed his hands to the earth that had absorbed the girl's blood.

A sharp, electrical pulse slammed the area between his eyes. His hands locked him in place.

She stared at him, her eyes bulging, her hands flaying at another's hands around her neck. Her mouth, fixed in a scream, gasped.

Noah's lips parted wide, stretching in a cry of pain and horror, his lungs wheezing.

Suddenly a snap of bone. Her eyes distended slightly, popping with shock as if she, too, heard the snap. The hands around her neck released their pressure.

Then, a high-pitched cry. Not hers lingering in the echo of time and space but an animalistic yowl from someone near her, a wail of dread and anguish.

Suddenly, Noah felt a cold, razor-sharp cut on his neck.

The slicing of her neck ripped jagged and deep. Those same hands that had strangled her life held a knife with a hooked end. He couldn't see the person's face, but he saw its shadow move down the girl's body and stab the knife through her clothing, ripping open her stomach.

A rage of thunder roared from overhead.

A jolt of energy came from out of the clouds. Noah was thrown from the spot.

His body lay convulsing.

When he opened his eyes, he recognized a streak of light moving from the clouds. Slicing through the gray, sheering away what was and what was not. Seen and not seen.

His heart thumped wildly from the girl's terror and his own.

Calming himself, he got up. He walked over to the prints Boggs showed him. From a dog? Large. Maybe seventy pounds. They could possibly be from a Labrador. Jake Cahill's dog. And then, as he explored further, scrutinizing each bit of dirt disturbed, each blade of grass bent, he came upon the prints he sought. Human. He put his hand to them.

An image came into his mind.

Human. But, not human.

Sad. Lonely. Afraid. Carrying a boy.

Noah got up and began to follow.

CHAPTER TWENTY-THREE: JAKE CAHILL

Jake thought it was Max Lamott because that was who he'd been thinking about. When the person came further in, he saw it wasn't Max.

"Teddy," Jake cried. "Oh, my God. Teddy, watch out." He nodded to the corner where IT squatted by the fire.

IT stood. It was half as tall as Teddy, and standing next to one another made the similarities hard to ignore. Both had long arms that hung closer to their knees than hips. Long fingers, the index finger the longest length, and thumb.

Jake knew Teddy had an illness causing his physical deformity. Unfortunately, his noticeable physical difference garnered him bullying all his life. So, does IT have the same disease? Jake wondered.

Teddy took off the Cardinals baseball cap he always wore. Hatless, his head, too, seemed much like IT's head. Only, Teddy had eyes and eyebrows. A nose and a mouth.

Teddy leaned and moved his head next to IT's head.

"Teddy, watch out," Jake shouted.

Teddy didn't respond. As if he hadn't heard Jake's warning.

For several minutes, the two stood in that manner. Jake was stymied. What were they doing? Why wasn't IT attacking Teddy? Then apparently finished, Teddy leaned back up and put his hat back on. IT squatted again by the fire.

Teddy walked over to Jake. His voice was high in tone and sometimes squeaked as if his vocal cords never changed like other boys. Jake thought it was because of his illness. The way he spoke was another reason why the kids persecuted him.

"He shouldn't have done this to you," Teddy said. "He was afraid." He began to untie the bindings.

"Afraid? IT killed Diddleman and Pitts." Jake grabbed Teddy. "If we don't get out of here, it's going to turn on us."

Teddy didn't answer. He returned to the fire. He removed his baseball cap again. But IT did not stand this time. IT seemed to be listening to him, although Jake could not hear Teddy talking. And Jake wasn't going to wait around for an explanation. Jake took off, "Run, Teddy!"

"DAAIDDIDIDDAWOOOOO. JAKKEEEEE."

Teddy twisted around before Jake moved but a few steps. He put out his hand. "Stop, Jake."

Jake's body froze in mid-stride. As if they were playing a game of Statue.

Teddy came over to Jake. "I am going to release you. Stay calm."

Teddy waved his hand in front of Jake. Jake fell to the ground. He looked up, stunned. "How did you do that?"

Jake couldn't believe what had just happened. How did Teddy turn him into something like ice? And he was cold.

IT hadn't moved. In fact, it remained in the same position, squatted in front of the fire, seemingly unconcerned with what was going on just a few feet away.

Jake lowered his voice. "I don't know how you know did...that, Teddy." He had no term for his body freezing. "But I've got to get out of here. Pitts...Diddleman..."

"Both are safe," Teddy said.

Jake shook his head. "There's their shirts." Jake pointed to the pile of rubbish. "And I remember seeing Pitts falling as if something hit him on the head." Again, his eyes landed on the blue from out the grey. "My sister. That's her blouse, Teddy." His voice choked from the thought of what IT may have done to his mother and sister.

"Johnny wouldn't hurt your sister or mother," Teddy assured him.

Jake's eyes took in Teddy's, unbelieving, unsure he could trust him. "Are you sure? Do you know where they are? Take me to them." And then, suddenly, his mind caught the name he'd heard.

"Johnny?" Jake looked over to IT next to the fire. As if IT was always cold. Of course, it had no clothes on, although it could have worn something from the rubbish pile.

"Wait here." Teddy started walking back out of the cave.

"Hold on. You're not going without me." Jake got up and started to follow.

Again, Teddy held out his hand.

Jake helplessly watched as Teddy continued in the direction he had come. When he returned, he had a girl with him. The girl stared at Jake hanging in midair. Then, when she glanced over to IT, she screamed and twisted around to run.

Only Teddy grabbed her before she got too far. He quietly said something to her. She calmed down. She nodded. Looked at IT, now not so much frightened as curious.

Teddy turned and waved his hand at Jake. And again, Jake fell to the floor.

"Will you quit doing that," Jake shouted. Dropping to the stone floor hurt. "Who is she?"

"She lived at the house," Teddy said.

"The house that burned? Do you know about it? I think my Dad was there. I think he was hurt in the fire."

The girl nodded. She turned to Teddy. "The man that saved me?"

"Okay, hold it." Jake struggled to get up, then thought better of it. He didn't want Teddy putting the freeze on him again. And how the heck was he doing that? "What do you mean, saved you?"

"This is Candela," Teddy said. "She was held prisoner in the house."

"By who?"

"By two men," Candela said. Her eyes filled and overflowed. "They hurt us."

"My Dad would never hurt anyone," Jake snapped, clenching his fists.

The girl blanched from his anger and stepped back.

Teddy shook his head. "No, Jake. Your father came to the house. It's how she escaped."

Jake was trying to take all this in. His mother and sister might be alive? His father saved this girl? Suddenly the image of the other girl's dead body came into his mind. "There was a girl by the house. She..."

Candela started sobbing. "Josie," she cried. "I saw one of the men kill her. Not the nicer man, the one who liked Josie. He told her he would take care of her. He was going to help her escape. But the other man. The mean one. The one who..." She broke out in sobs. "Who would beat us."

Teddy put his arm around her. "You're safe now. You're safe here."

Jake said, "I'm going to stand up now, Teddy."

Teddy nodded.

Jake stood. The pieces were still a puzzle. "You said Diddleman and Pitts are safe."

"Diddleman told Sheriff Boggs," Teddy said. "I took Pitts to the hospital."

"But I saw Oliver fall, hurt."

"He's okay. I think he fainted." He glanced back to where they had entered. Then, he said quietly, "They're looking for us."

"You mean, Sheriff Boggs is looking for us? Great. Let's go." Jake looked over to the fire pit. "But what about IT? I mean, Johnny?"

Johnny was watching the group. Could it understand what they were saying?

Teddy said. "Other men, not the police, are hunting for us. They want to hurt me. And," he glanced over at Johnny, "They will kill my brother."

CHAPTER TWENTY-FOUR: SHERIFF BOGGS

Standwick radioed Boggs, informing him the search team was combing a large area around Summit Trail.

"Deputy Warner is coordinating," Standwick said. "She knows the territory best."

"I agree," Boggs answered.

"Between all of us, we've gathered almost fifty county, state and local police, and park personnel, as well as citizens who volunteered."

"Good job. I should be there in ten."

"Copy that." Standwick signed off.

As Boggs drove, he thought of what Duel said: "There wasn't any blood." Which would not necessarily strike him as being out of the ordinary. The animal could have bled out. But Riker said, "Bloodless. Not one drop."

Before he'd left, Boggs asked Riker not to do any more animal incinerations. And if other animals were found in the same condition, he asked to be notified immediately.

Driving, Boggs thought back again to the deer. The deer were bloody, not bloodless. The two didn't sound like the same set of circumstances.

Could this be some sort of cult practice? Boggs had read an article about cattle mutilations in Oregon where cows' utters and genitals were cut off. The investigation's theory was that devil-worshipers had perpetuated the brutality. Although, the article also mentioned some conspiracy theorists argued aliens had done the mutilations.

Aliens, he scoffed. Why would someone from another planet, who could get to earth from a million light-years away, want a cow's utter? Nonsense.

He remembered then back to a time in Vietnam. He and another guy were sitting in camp, drinking and telling tales. The dude told him he had a story Boggs could never top. How his flight squad came across what looked like two saucer-shaped objects out from the China Sea. They radioed in and were ordered to follow. Further out, the squad found themselves outnumbered. Thirty, forty, maybe a hundred of them.

"I could get killed telling you this," he had said, his hand trembling, and not just from the beer he was holding. "When we reported in, we were ordered immediately back. Some bigwigs came into camp the next day and questioned us. Then we were told we didn't see anything. That what we saw was weather balloons that the navy let loose."

He said, "What I saw wasn't any balloon."

In his story, Walter's claim of aliens was adding tinder to the fire. People didn't like what they didn't understand. And even though most knew Tira had taken her son to doctors and told people Ted suffered from a disease, Boggs knew they still didn't like the way Teddy looked. Add to his looks, they didn't like his sharp mind and felt threatened by him.

Boggs was determined to squash Forester's madness in thinking Ted had anything to do with Jake and Oliver's missing.

He pulled into the Eagles Park entrance just as dispatch called on his radio. Oliver Pitts had been admitted to Pinkerton General. Unfortunately, the dispatcher didn't have a status on Jake.

Boggs made a quick U-turn. He punched on his lights and siren. Good news.

He considered calling Standwick and canceling the search but decided he'd better wait. If Jake wasn't with Oliver, then Oliver might be able to tell them where to find Jake. Then, the search party could pinpoint and locate him.

Thunder rolled overhead.

The sky lit with a flash of lightning.

As Boggs turned into Pinkerton General Hospital, he saw someone standing on the corner.

Ted Templeton.

Beside him stood a large, brown Labrador.

CHAPTER TWENTY-FIVE: CHIEF MOORE

Moore picked up his phone.

"It's me, Chief," Hayworth said.

"What do you want?" Moore sniped.

"I've been watching the Fed like you told me. I followed him to Eagl es and saw him talking to Chatan Lamott."

Moore didn't respond, but his mind was whirling. How did the Fed find Lamott? Instead, Moore had seen Lamott several times walking near the house.

Potter needed to be handled.

"Why do you think he wanted to talk to Chatan, Chief?" Hayworth asked, thinking aloud.

"How the hell do I know?" Moore barked. "What I want to know is who else is he talking to."

"Should I follow Chatan?"

"Not him, you idiot," Moore snapped. "Although knowing who else Lamott might be talking to could be valuable. He said, "I want your eyes on that Fed. And what about Boggs?"

"No intel on him at the moment, Chief. I thought the Fed would be the priority."

For once, the idiot was right. Moore said, "Don't be doing your own thinking. I don't want that Fed out of your sight. You got that?"

"Copy that," Hayworth responded. Again, as if thinking aloud, "But, I still can't figure out how the Fed and Chatan Lamott got so chummy."

"What do you mean, chummy?"

"Wellllll," Hayworth drew the word out. "I'm thinking this here Fed isn't from around these parts. So how would he know Lamott hangs out in these woods? The Fed went straight over to this area, a ways from the dock. Nothing there that I could see. And as soon as the Fed got there, ol'Chatan comes walking out from the bushes like some kind of mountaineer man." Hayworth paused, then added, "Although he claims to be Indian. I don't remember what kind of Indian, maybe..."

Moore breathed fire. "Listen to me. I don't pay you to think. Just follow and report back to me."

If Moore had waited one more second, he would have heard Hayworth respond, "It was almost as if Chatan was in the bushes waiting for the guy to show up." But Moore already ended the call.

Moore barely slammed the phone down when it rang again. "Damn it, Hayworth."

"Not Hayworth by a long shot," said the voice on the other end of the line.

"What do you want?"

"I thought you'd want to know. I just checked Oliver Pitts into the hospital," Potter said.

"When did this happen?" Moore growled.

"Maybe twenty minutes. A half-hour."

"Is Cahill's kid there, too?"

"No." Potter said, "I don't like this Purvis. I don't like this at all." His voice lowered. "And .....I can't quit thinking about how you..."

"Get your head out of your ass," Moore demanded. "I did what had to be done. And don't think you're not in this as deep as I am." Then, his voice lowered to that of a snarling dog's, "What's the kid told them?"

"Nothing of any consequence. Yet." Potter assured him.

"Sedate him."

"I tried, but Matt Oliver refused to let me. He claims his kid said he needs to talk to the Sheriff."

Mentioning Boggs deepened Moore's growl. "Demand it. Say it's necessary for medical reasons." Then Moore grilled, "What could Cahill have told his kid?"

Potter's voice grew jittery. "I told you. I had Cahill heavily sedated. He was out of it. He didn't recognize me. I'm sure the Pitts kid doesn't know anything.

"Those three boys didn't go up to Point House on a whim. Cahill had to have told his kid something. What?"

Potter balked. "I tell you, the guy was dying."

"If you don't want the needle, you'd better hope he didn't say anything. If you wouldn't have..."

"Hey," Potter argued. "It wasn't me who..."

Moore exploded. "If you know what's good for you, find out how much this Pitts' kid knows."

"Are you threatening me, Purvis? After what you did?"

Moore licked his lips, thinking about the girl from the house. Potter's girl. If Purvis had known what a hellcat she was, he never would have allowed Potter to claim her. Potter treated the girl like she was a damn virgin.

Moore said, "Cahill was your responsibility, not mine. Remember that?" He paused, hearing no response from Potter. "You took care of Cahill, right?"

Potter didn't answer.

"Put a needle in that kid's arm before Boggs gets to him." Moore hung up, wondering how much longer he could trust Potter. Maybe not long, he thought.

There had been six girls left in the house. They had once held as many as twelve girls in the beginning. He and Potter had made a tidy sum satisfying the tastes of those like him who wanted a bit more "excitement" in their lives. Who, like him, enjoyed the chase as much as the conquest. Unlike Potter, Moore didn't get emotionally involved. He never saw any of the girls other than what they were, a means to an end.

The idea of creating a private club, Point House, where men could fulfill their sexual fantasies without persecution came to him when he stopped a Hispanic girl at the bus station. She didn't speak much English and held only an address of what she understood to be a job. She had all the markers of an illegal. No language. Clothes, cast-off Walmart specials. He didn't learn until later that she confused Pinkerton with Postville. A town known for hiring illegals for its kosher slaughterhouse and meatpacking.

Young. She couldn't have been more than thirteen, fourteen. Raven black hair she finger-brushed off a face of large brown eyes, heavy lashes, and pink lips.

He remembered how her lips trembled when he put her into the back of his SUV. How the tears flowed off her brown, youthful skin. She trembled like an antelope cornered. And he felt like a roaring lion.

Without thinking, no real plan, he drove to Eagles Park. It was off-season. A few out fishing, but no one camping. "Te estoy hablando al hotel," he said in what he could remember from his high school Spanish classes. "Limpiea interna." All the while, he led her up the Summit Trail.

When he got her to the junction of Summit Trail, and she saw no hotel, she tried to run. He gave chase, his adrenaline surging with each sweet scream from her small, pink lips.

He caught her. Dragged her along the trail to the point where he knew it swerved off. A trail that led to an abandoned cabin.

When he pushed her inside, she tried to run again. He cornered her. Toyed with her. And when he took her, her screams became lost to the woods, to the world she had left, and the new life she would never reach. He mounted her, each thrust filling him with absolute power.

He took her again and again—day after day. And then, the idea formed. There had to be other men like him. Men with needs unfulfilled.

He kidnapped more girls he found waiting to change buses at the station. He brought them to the house, which he called Point House. His first guest was Potter. He needed Potter to come up to handle injuries with one girl after he had gotten a little rough. Soon there were others injured. So Potter became a permanent guest. He also provided the ease of getting up to Point House with the use of AirCare. A fee paid to a satisfied pilot.

Point House became a good business. Girls could be easily replaced. No one missed those coming into the country illegally. A handful of men who joined in the fun understood if the secret was ever found out, they would all spend the rest of their lives in prison.

It was all working perfectly until Cahill came snooping around looking for his wife and daughter. One of the girls charged out the door while Moore tried to get rid of him. She cried out for help. And in the chaos of getting her back in, another girl ran out. And then another.

He knocked Cahill out and tied him up. And to destroy any finger-pointing by the escaped girls on the chance they were picked up, he made his decision to get rid of Point House.

By the time Potter got there, Moore was splashing the house with gasoline. He was surprised to see one of the girls with him. Had Potter stupidly taken the girl back to Pinkerton with him? Moore knew he had taken her once before, and when Moore caught him, he had told Potter his freakish need to try to develop some sort of relationship was off the wall stupid.

As the inferno burned wood to ash, Potter talked about how he would take care of the girl. He argued that Moore didn't need to worry. She would never say anything. Moore could trust him to keep her secreted away.

Moore grabbed ahold of Potter and gave him a good shaking. The girl tried to run. Moore caught her. As Potter tried to pry him off her, Moore's fingers clamped down like a vise around her throat. Shut off her screams. Her breath. And even though he heard the break of bone, he couldn't stop. Then, wanting to make sure she was dead, he grabbed the hunting knife he carried in his boot, and he slit the girl's throat. Then, he ripped her open like the deer he had seen on the trail.

Potter swore he would never forgive him. But Moore reminded Potter the same could easily happen to him.

That same day, the storm coursed through Pinkerton. Then, several days later, someone found Cahill along the highway. And now, two boys were missing.

It was all unraveling.

Someone knocked at his office door. "What is it?" Moore barked.

The door opened, and Acting-Commander Jim Rants popped his head in. "I thought you'd want to know the Pitts kid showed up."

"Tell me something I don't know," Moore countered. "Now close that damn door. I have work to do."

CHAPTER TWENTY-SIX: SHERIFF BOGGS

Boggs saw Dr. Potter standing at the floor desk writing in a medical file. "How is he?" Boggs asked.

"He needs rest," Potter closed the file. "They wouldn't let me sedate him until you got here, and I suggest you keep your visit short. The boy's in shock."

"Any serious injuries?" Boggs asked.

"Nothing that won't mend. He wouldn't tell me what happened. Maybe you'll be able to get it out of him."

"I intend to," Boggs said.

"He's in room 210." Potter led him down the corridor.

On entering, Boggs saw Matt Pitts in a chair over by the window, half-sleep. From relief as well as the lack of sleep, Boggs figured. Katherine Pitts sat by her son, holding his hand. She looked up and smiled. She, too, was relieved to have her son back and not severely injured.

Oliver sat up in bed, his eyes wide with relief. "Sheriff?"

Matt woke. "Look who decided to come home," he joked to Boggs, offering a happy grin.

"It's good to have you home," Boggs said to Oliver.

The boy reached over to the stand next to his bed and grabbed his glasses. Other than weary, he appeared fine.

Oliver said, "I wish Jake was here with me. We need to find him."

"Then he wasn't with you?"

Oliver shook his head.

Matthew offered, "Oliver said Ted Templeton found him and brought him to the hospital. Ted should be the one you talk to."

Was that why Ted was waiting at the corner? Boggs wondered. Was he waiting to inform the police where he had found Oliver so that they could search for Jake?

"I plan to as soon as I have a chance to speak to Oliver."

"I need to talk to the Sheriff alone," Oliver told his parents.

"Now, Oliver," Matt cautioned. He said to Boggs, "Can't this wait? He needs to get some rest."

"I told you, Dad," Oliver returned not only to his father but to everyone in the room. "Jake's dad said to only speak to Sheriff Boggs."

Boggs noticed how Oliver's eyes settled on something beyond Boggs' shoulder.

"I thought you said you didn't know where you were found," his dad said.

"I don't." Oliver thought a minute. "Or I'm not sure. Ted knows. He found me."

Glancing over his shoulder, Boggs saw Dr. Potter standing on the threshold. Neither in nor out.

Oliver said, again to Boggs more than the others, "Jake's dad was here in the hospital." He glanced at his mother. "You told Jake his dad was here."

Katherine colored slightly, and she glanced to the doorway. She shook her head. "No. I was mistaken." She sighed, "Oh, god. If I am the cause of any of this." She leaned over and hugged her son. "I am so sorry, Oliver. I was wrong. It was another man who was injured." She said to the Boggs. "With Jake's dad missing, and the burn victim similar in appearance, I guess I assumed it was Jake's dad. I should have been certain first."

Katherine Pitts didn't come across to Boggs as someone who would make assumptions.

"You weren't wrong, Mom," Oliver stated firmly. "I believe Jake, no matter what Dr. Potter says."

Dr. Potter cleared his throat. "I told you, son, the burn victim was from a truck overturning on the highway." Then, he said to Boggs, "The poor guy was burned on seventy-five percent of his body. Badly disfigured. Jake couldn't have recognized him. The man couldn't speak. How he survived long enough for someone to discover him along the highway was amazing."

He continued, "We had no way of checking his identity, and he needed services beyond what we could give him here. So I had him immediately sent to the University's burn center."

Boggs' brow hurled. Immediately? Different than what Potter told him up at the crime scene. And not so quick that three boys heard about his being in the hospital and came to see if it was Jake's dad.

Again, he made a mental note to call the Iowa University Burn Unit and see when the patient transfer occurred. Something he wanted to do earlier, but events were moving faster than he could catch up.

Potter added, "I received news shortly after he arrived that he didn't survive his injuries."

Boggs added this to his other mental notations. He needed to contact the City of Iowa's coroner. They would have attempted to get fingerprints or dental records for identification.

Oliver shouted. "He can't die. Not until we find Jake's mom and sister." His chin quivered, "He's all Jake has left."

"Oh, Jake," his mom wrapped her arms around him.

Dr. Potter moved in and over to the bed. "As you can see, Oliver needs his rest."

"Yes," Katherine Pitts agreed.

Dr. Potter called the nurse and ordered some medication.

Oliver pulled off his glasses and brushed the tears off his face. Sitting up straight and tall, he proclaimed, "You will not put me asleep. Not yet. Not until I've spoken to Sheriff Boggs." He emphasized, "Alone."

"But right after?" his mother sought his agreement. "Dr. Potter's right, Oliver. You need to get some rest."

Oliver's stamina to remain steadfastness faded in his shoulders, but his face held firm. He nodded. "I promise."

Katherine got up out of her chair. She came over to Boggs, "Not for long, please."

Boggs nodded. "I only have a couple of questions."

Boggs waited for Matt and Katherine, and a reluctant Dr. Potter to leave the room.

"Shut the door, please," Oliver said.

Boggs did so. Then he went over and took the chair Oliver's mother vacated. "Okay, start from the beginning if you can."

Oliver told Boggs the events leading up to their decision to go to Eagles Park. About their visit to the hospital in search of Jake's dad.

"Why don't you believe Dr. Potter?" Boggs asked.

"Ask my mother when Dr. Potter's not around," Oliver returned sharply. "I don't think she does, either."

Boggs intended to talk with her and Matt alone as soon as he got the chance.

Oliver was methodical in the telling, leaving out few details. Or at least there were no inconsistencies from what Walter told. When he got to the point of having seen the first dead deer, his recalled observations matched Boggs'. The only difference between Walter and Oliver's stories came at the moment when Walter said they saw what Walter described as an alien.

"Then we saw this strange person. Or what I thought at first was a person, but I immediately identified it as an alien."

Hearing Walter use the term caused Boggs to agree with Office Hayworth. A little storytelling may have invaded the facts. It could happen in recall. But Oliver using the word? Boggs knew Oliver was an honor student. And, he'd heard how the boy had won several Rubik's Cube contests. A fact to be admired, at least by Boggs, since when he tried to play with the puzzle, he ended up throwing the cube against the wall in exasperation.

While Walter started out saying it was an alien, he'd changed his mind and identified what he saw as Ted. Boggs said to Oliver, "Walter said he thought it was Ted Templeton."

Rubbing the back of his head, Oliver gave the statement some thought. "I can see why he said that. Teddy likes us, and he's usually around somewhere. Not that we do stuff with him. And, I'm not saying we wouldn't. Walter doesn't like him much, but Teddy really likes Jake, and I have no problems with him. But he's a bit on the shy side. He likes being on the sidelines."

He continued. "Yeah, I can see why Walter thought it was Ted. But it'd have to be a naked Teddy Templeton. And a whole lot smaller. The alien wasn't wearing any clothes."

"What?" Identification was an exceptional detail in an investigation. Unfortunately, Walter had forgotten to mention this detail.

"It's male. I'd say it stood shorter than five feet. And heavy around the middle. The body's trunk was longer, and it had short legs. Its feet were strange. It was as if they were flippers or hooves, not feet." He took a beat, then said, "It wasn't human. Not really. Its skin was strange. Grey-colored."

Boggs commented. "That's a surprisingly good detail. How can you be so sure of your description? Walter said when it saw you guys, it ran. Are you saying that this...." He wasn't sure what to call it, person, animal? Alien?

Oliver smiled. "I have a photographic memory. Details stick with me. I think it's why I am so good with the cube. My mind remembers and analyzes the last position while I am spinning to the next."

He went on. "Actually, we saw it twice. Once by one of the dead deer and then by the burned cabin next to the girl."

"Weren't you scared?" Boggs asked. "If I would have seen a possible alien from another planet, I think I would have hightailed it out of there."

The boy shook his head. "Jake and I have been studying the Greys for a long time. The Greys are a type of alien."

"Where have you been reading about them?"

"There are books about people who have had eye-witness accounts." Again, he paused a beat, "And been abducted."

There we go, Boggs thought.

Oliver must have noticed the skepticism in Boggs' face. "I know it doesn't sound logical, Sheriff. But, if you give it some thought, it really does make logical sense. Voyager 2 is giving back new information on our solar system. Scientists are saying that there may be many more planets in the Milky Way that we haven't discovered" He emphasized, "If we don't know much about our own galaxy, then how can we be sure about the rest of the universe?"

He continued. "I've read a whole lot. I love astronomy and mathematics. And I have never read of a Grey killing anyone. Have you? Have you read any newspaper article where someone was killed by an alien?"

The only knowledge Boggs held on the subject came from sensational tabloids in the rack by the grocery checkout. *Woman has alien's baby.*

"It doesn't make logical sense to me, Oliver. And it doesn't explain what happened to you boys."

Oliver tried again. "It does make sense. Jake and I track alien sightings on the Internet. He's into them like I am. And you know, Jake's dad once worked for Nasa." He took a breath. "I don't know what happened to Jake's dad. Maybe he frightened them, and they used a laser gun on him or something."

"You saw more than one?" Boggs asked, new information.

"No, just the one. But Jake saw his mom and sister taken up into a spaceship during the tornado. And I'd been researching and found a site following the storms in the Midwest linking them to UFO sightings. It's how they're coming here, Sheriff. They're hiding in the storms."

This is getting us nowhere, Boggs thought. And seeing the slump of Oliver's shoulders and the sheen of sweat on his forehead, he knew he had to wrap up the conversation.

"Okay," Boggs said. "Let's say what you saw is true. What happened then? Did it try to attack you guys?"

"No," Oliver said emphatically. "We didn't threaten it. You aren't listening. They aren't any more aggressive than we are. They are like us. They may have even been us once. Maybe earth was even their home at one point if they are time travelers. And they are coming back to understand their origins."

The expression of skepticism Boggs felt must have formed on his face.

"Jake thought it might be able to lead him to his mom and sister." He paused, his voice lowering. "And then..." He pressed his forehead with the heel of his hand.

"Do you want me to bring in your mom and dad?" Boggs was worried he was pushing the boy too far. "Do you need to rest for a few minutes?"

"No," Oliver answered firmly. He resettled himself taller in the bed. "We followed it. Well, more like chased it. At least from its perspective. It may have thought we were after it.

"As we ran, I began smelling smoke. I thought it was from a campfire. Only, I knew campfires weren't allowed in the park. Because of fires."

He didn't wait for Boggs' acknowledgment. "The smell of smoke got stronger, and then we broke through into this clearing where there was a burned cabin. The alien was standing by it. And there was a body."

His voice lowered as if he were back, remembering, "Jake's screaming at it. I think he thought the body was his mom or his sister Shilo. And then it took off running again.

"We went over to where the body was. It was a girl. And she'd been killed. But not by it. I'm pretty sure. The deer were killed differently than this girl. It may have killed the deer, but not her, I bet."

He stopped. "Next thing I knew, I was in a cave. And Teddy was there. I was dizzy, and I couldn't walk."

"Was Jake there, too?"

"I don't think so," Oliver said. Then added, "But I can tell you one thing."

"What's that?"

"I don't think Teddy saved my life. I don't think I was in danger. I never felt like I was. I'm not sure how he found me. But Teddy carried me all the way back down the trail. And that's a long way. He wouldn't let me try to walk. He said he was taking me back home. That I was going to be okay. And when I asked about Jake and Diddleman, he said not to worry. They were okay too."

Boggs found Oliver's parents at the nurse's desk. Dr. Potter was there.

"What did the boy tell you?" Potter was the first to ask.

"You can give Oliver something to help him sleep now." Then, he addressed Oliver's parents. "I would like to speak with you a little later if we can. May I stop by your place in a couple of hours?"

"Of course," Matt said. "Although, I'm sure I won't get Katherine an inch away from Oliver's bed, asleep or not."

"Understandable." Boggs reached out and put his hand to Katherine's arm. "You have a remarkable boy, there."

"Us we do," she smiled. "If you give us a time, I will come back to the house so that we talk."

Boggs noticed how her eyes moved across his shoulder to where Dr. Potter still stood, apparently giving a nurse instruction on medication.

When Boggs left, he thought he'd go find Ted. Oliver hadn't mentioned the dog. And he wasn't sure how to take Oliver's story. The bit about an alien, of course, was an exaggeration. But Walter and Oliver gave the same description. And what they described didn't sound human. An animal?"

Ted Templeton was nowhere to be seen.

Boggs knew he had to find him. If Ted found Oliver, maybe he knew where Jake was, too. And if Bill Cahill was the burn victim in the hospital, had he died as Potter claimed of the man he MedVac'd to Iowa City? Why was Potter lying?

CHAPTER TWENTY-SEVEN: CHIEF MOORE

Purvis Moore sat at his desk, his hands clenched fiercely together.

It was unraveling. Because of Bill Cahill. A nobody.

And Potter? The man needed to be taken care of as well. He wasn't following orders. He was miscalculating how much Moore would put up with. All over some silly, illegal. "His girl," Potter had said.

Purvis laughed. He created the club. He stretched his neck to gather the girls. What did Potter do other than make more money than he ever could as a small-town doctor?

His girl. They were all MY girls.

He vaulted from his desk. Kicked away his chair. Teeth grinding, mouth squeezed to keep from raging, each breath heavy in his gut before exploding from his lungs. He paced, hands clenching and unclenching until new thoughts pushed away the old. His brain flooded with answers to his predicament. Genius, he claimed aloud to that part of himself that always found a way. And it would be so easy.

He laughed. "Easy," he exclaimed. "Perfect."

He went back to his desk. Sat and relaxed. The answer, Ted Templeton. Of course.

Moore smiled. What causes fear faster than death? Finding another body murdered will cause everyone to forget about Jake Cahill.

Moore's thoughts went back to the girls who'd escaped. He'd learned about two of them. Now, where was the third?

He wiggled his fingers as if all his ideas were right in front of him. As if someone sat on the other side of the desk offering suggestions that were up for Moore's taking.

Right. Pinkerton doesn't have an alien killing girls. Ted Templeton is killing them.

Ah, huh, he smiled. Nodded his agreement. I do surprise myself sometimes. It doesn't matter who or where. Finding another murdered girl will ramp up the fear beyond what Boggs or that Fed can control.

"A mob can't be stopped," he said aloud.

Fear surpasses belief, he heard.

"You're right there."

Maybe he would find a way to get rid of Boggs, too.

"We need to deal with Boggs," he said.

You're right there, he heard.

Without Boggs, he reasoned, he'd have free reign until a new Sheriff was brought in. Time enough to maybe replace what was lost. Another house? Why the hell not? In fact, perhaps he'd give the new Sheriff a free membership.

And why not deal with Potter as well as Boggs? Potter was no longer an asset.

He waved his hand as if dismissing the discussion.

He reached for his phone. Dialed the home of Doug Forester. "Doug. I've been thinking about what you said. I think we should meet. Walter's story is beginning to make sense to me."

He listened. Sucked his bottom lip. "Yep. I agree. I might need some help, though. You interested in getting a beer?"

CHAPTER TWENTY-EIGHT: MAJOR SEARS

Noah followed his intuitive trail until suddenly it abruptly ended.

As final as a door shutting closed. The deadbolt shoved into place.

The brush had thickened. Low Oak tree branches made going farther hard. A gulch scored the earth from the rain gushing off the hillside. Maybe also washing way other tracks.

The wind was picking up. The clouds grumbled. Noah felt a drop of rain.

He took an eye-map of where he was to lead Boggs's search party back to the area. He needed to warn them of the terrain. They would need tools to clear away some of the brush. There was something here. He was sure of it.

Although maybe he should come back on his own. What he might find may not only be Jake Cahill.

He let the rain fall on him. A heavy mist, really, not rain yet. But the clouds were squeezing together, combining power, threatening.

He cleared his mind. Gave a hard listen. The word safe came into his thoughts. The boy was safe. For now.

Making his way back to the crime scene, he took the same trail back to the lake and to his car. On the way into town, he saw a City SUV pull out of the Hoof and Beer parking lot. Chief of Police labeled on its side.

Reminding himself that he hadn't eaten, he pulled into the space emptied.

CHAPTER TWENTY-NINE: OFFICER HAYWORTH

Officer Hayworth found two things interesting.

The first was spotting Chief Moore's SUV leaving the Hoof and Beer parking lot. The Chief never frequented the bar as far as Hayworth knew. In fact, more than once, the Chief openly remarked how the place needed to be torn down. Saying it was a sore sight on the way into the park and gathered riffraff.

The second was seeing the Fed slow down as the Chief pulled out of the lot.

The two simultaneous incidents vexed him. He fretted about what he should do. Should he call the Chief and tell him that the Fed was going into the same place he'd just left? Or should he wait? Find out why the Fed was going there?

After the Fed had gone inside, Hayworth pulled into the lot and sat staring at the bar's door. If having the Fed stop directly after the Chief left was totally a coincidence, then his job was to follow the Fed. But those in the bar might get jittery having just had the Chief of Police visit and then straight behind him another policeman. Probably most inside were wanted for one thing or another. Traffic warrants. Unpaid child support. Drugs.

He also didn't want the Fed figuring out he was being followed.

Hayworth sat for several minutes, gnawing on his cheek. What if the Fed just stopped for directions?

When it was apparent the Fed wasn't coming back out, Hayworth pulled around the back of the bar. He opened the car's trunk. He kept some extra clothing in here in case he found time to take a moment or two out for some fishing. Slow days weren't easy to get through.

Hayworth had visited Ed's Hoof and Beer once or twice. After all, it was his job to be aware of those who might churn up trouble. He used to patrol at the border of City Limits and County, ticketing those coming back into town from the bar, until the mayor started screaming entrapment when Hayworth stopped him for a breath test. The Chief screamed at him for over an hour for that one.

Hayworth removed his official cap. Brushed it off carefully and placed it in the trunk where it couldn't get dirty. He took off his duty belt. He felt naked without the heaviness on his hips. Only, leaving his gun was out of the question. The Hoof and Beer was rough. And he prided himself on always being ready to maintain the peace. No matter the circumstance. He extracted it from its holster.

He exchanged his uniform pants for stained ones. He took off his official shirt and slipped into an old one, and over it, a fishing vest with pockets.

He glanced around for nosey-noosers not minding their own business. No one. Patrons only went through the front door. If someone came out back, it might only be the owner, Al. An Ed hadn't owned the place in years.

He slipped his gun into his pants behind the fishing vest. Like he'd seen them do on cop shows. Ready if needed. He pulled out a battered cap with a trout stitched on the front. Pulling it low on his head, the bill shading his eyes, he closed the trunk lid. Again, he checked to see if anyone had been watching him. Then, he hunkered his shoulders and made his way into the bar.

It took a moment for his eyes to adjust. The stuffed animal heads on the wall over the bar stared as he entered. When his eyes adjusted, he saw a couple of guys turn on their seats in his direction—No-gooders, by his judgment.

The bartender moved across and said something to one of the men. The two men laughed, pushed their glasses forward, and quickly forgot someone new had entered.

Hayworth sucked on his front teeth. For the first time in a long while, he felt as if he had come into his own. His hands reached to his hips as if to pull up his duty belt. He inhaled, feeling the bulk of the gun at his back. He'd always wanted to work undercover. If he did a good job, the Chief might move him up to detective.

He saw the Fed several stools down from the men who were now drinking the new beers put before them. There was an empty stool next to him. Hayworth sauntered over. He was just a man coming back from fishing needing a cold one.

CHAPTER THIRTY: MAJOR SEARS

Dark. Smelling of stale popcorn and spilled beer.

A plank of finely jeweled burl wood ran the length of the room lined with well-worn, red vinyl stools. Heads of antlered deer, glassy-eyed, held center court. Across from the bar, small booths covered in the same-colored vinyl ran the length of the room to its end. He saw how the booths were separated with wooden barriers holding glass cases of taxidermized animals. Raccoons held up paws in running postures. Squirrels were customed dressed in vignettes, like The Three Stooges.

Noah took an empty stool.

"What can I get you," the bar man asked, wiping the counter with a rag several shades beyond its original white.

Noah glanced around for a menu. Then, seeing none and determining one wasn't going to be offered, he spotted someone down biting into a hamburger.

"I'll have a burger."

"Beef or Bison?" The barman asked.

"Beef."

"Want a beer with that?"

"Whatever you've got on tap."

"Bud, okay?

"Bud's fine."

As the barman left to claim his order, someone took the empty seat next to him.

The bartender put a glass of frothing amber liquid in front of Noah. Then he moved to the next guy asking him what he wanted.

"New around here?"

It took a moment for Noah to realize it was the man who had taken the empty stool. With his cap so low over his eyes, Noah could only see the man's weak chin beneath a pointy nose.

"Just visiting," Noah replied.

"You came to the right place," the man said. "If you're looking for some hiking and camping, that is." He paused, "Where're you from?"

Noah was interrupted from replying by raised voices stirring behind him.

He saw Doug Forester standing outside a booth holding center court.

"That's what I said." Forester leaned a bit like the Tower of Pisa. His eyes were bloodshot. "Chief Moore came in to personally tell me the Pitts kid is back and that Ted Templeton had something to do with his missing."

Stools squeaked, and vinyl rubbed as customers swiveled away from their beers. Several commenting:

"Told you so."

"About damn time."

A murmur of voice like leaves in wind rattling from the booths.

"What about the other kid?" Someone from the booths shouted.

"Well, that's the thing." Forester shook his head, lowering his eyes to the floor as if the information he was about to impart was hard to deliver. "Now, this was told to me on a confidential nature, and I should keep it to myself. But seeing all of us are concerned about what's not right here, I think it's best to pass on what I know. It was only the Pitts kid who showed up. Maybe the Cahill kid ain't able to."

The mummer picked up, carrying whispered questions to those closest.

"Are you saying the Cahill kid may be dead?" Someone from the stools yelled.

Forester raised his hand. "I'm not saying. Or should I say, I've been told to keep what information I have confidential? But I can tell you Chief Moore said I should keep my Walter close at hand.

And, he said he felt that the news in the next few days may not get any better."

He let that hang.

"I'm here to tell you, and you can take this to the bank. I'm not letting that Templeton kid anywhere near my own. I can't be responsible for what I might do. If the police can't control this situation, I will."

Voices rose. "He better not come near my place."

"That retard's dangerous. I've said so many a time."

"Maybe we should take care of him before someone else gets killed."

The last came from the back. Noah thought it sounded like the same person who asked if Jake Cahill was dead.

Forester feigned making the decision. "Do what you think fit. Right now, I'm going home and make sure my boy's safe."

He left the bar.

Once the door shut behind him, voices chorused into a volume of concern. Several stated they were also going home to see about theirs, trailing Forester out the door, shouting Forester's name. "Hey Doug, wait up."

"Pitts' kid's been found?" The question came from the man sitting next to him. "Why'd the Chief come to tell Forester?"

Noah glanced at the man. The man's eyes widened further seeing Noah's notice as if surprised by what had come out of his mouth. He swiveled around quickly, giving Noah his back, and began fidgeting with his untouched beer.

One of Chief Moore's men. How long had he been following him?

The bartender set Noah's hamburger down in front of him. Noah pulled out his billfold and placed some money on the bar.

CHAPTER THIRTY-ONE: SHERIFF BOGGS

Standwick's cruiser was in the lot, and beside it was park manager Deputy Elizabeth Warner's vehicle.

Mespelt greeted Boggs as he walked into the lobby, "One down, one to go," he said, remarking on Oliver Pitts being back home.

Boggs nodded. "Soon, I hope. This storm is going to break. We need to find that boy before it does."

"The weatherman's saying it's building up. It may be as bad as the last one. Tornado warnings."

"We can't take much more bad news." Boggs moved through the pass-way. "Standwick in his office?"

"With Warner," Mesplet said. He added, "I heard back on those handcuffs found at the site. The City ordered them about five or six years ago."

"Good to know. Thanks." Boggs doubted they came from the City unless an officer had been up there and dropped them.

Boggs picked up his phone and called the Iowa City Coroner's office only to be told what Potter had said. The person sent to them had died on arrival from Pinkerton. They still had no ID. Fingerprinting was impossible due to the amount of damage to his hands, but dental imprints were processed through the National Persons System.

NMUPS was a database containing DNA, dental charts, skeletal X-rays, and other distinguishable details about unidentified persons. Families of those missing, law enforcement agencies, and others provided much of the database. Boggs didn't have access to the database, but a larger police force or the FBI would. But, unless there was a record on Cahill, the victim may never be ID'd.

"We may have a missing person here. Look for information on William or Bill Cahill. He's
worked for NASA. You should find something if it's him."

After he'd made the call, Boggs went to Standwick's office where he found Standwick and Warner studying a topographical map of Eagles Park. Both looked up as Boggs came in.

"Elizabeth," Boggs greeted. He asked Standwick, "How's the search going?"

Standwick said, "We've covered the area where the boys were last seen fairly good. A larger team is looking in parallel areas. We have doubled the volunteers we had this morning. Elizabeth and I are trying to decide where to look next."

Boggs said, "I guess you've heard Ted Templeton carried Oliver Pitts back to town? Oliver couldn't tell me where he was when Ted found him, but Ted couldn't have carried him too far." He asked Elizabeth. "What are your thoughts on this?"

Elizabeth Warner's hair, streaked with highlights of grey, hung loosely down her back. Smile lines from seeing Boggs turned to concern. "Clarence and I agree. He must have found him close by the Summit Trail. Ted couldn't have carried him far."

"Oliver said he thought he woke up in a cave," Boggs told them. "You might want to talk to him when he wakes up, Elizabeth.
You may be able to describe some areas that will trigger his memory." He added, "They've given him something to rest right now."

"Cave," Elizabeth quietly repeated. "She pointed on the map." She said to Standwick. "There are some small, shallow caves in this area. Not far from where they were last seen."

She looked up to Boggs, "And Jake?"

Boggs shook his head. "Oliver said he didn't think Jake was in the same place."

"Still," Elizabeth said. She again eyed the map. "We can go into this area and then move over this way..." Her finger pointed out a direction.

"Keep me informed," Boggs said. "I need to find Ted Templeton. He may have all our answers." He left for his office just as Mespelt came looking for him. "That federal agent Sears is here to see you."

Boggs sighed. He didn't need Sears' disruption right now. There was still a boy's life at risk. And he needed to talk to Ted's mother.

He moved into his office. His stomach growled seeing the unwrapped sandwich he'd picked up from Sally's on his way back to the station. He opened the top drawer of his desk and shoved it in—no time to eat.

CHAPTER THIRTY TWO

"I thought I should update you on what I've learned," Sears said, walking into Boggs'office.

"If you found something, I hope to hell it's Jake Cahill. Once we find him, we're at the tail-end of all this."

"I'm not so sure about that." Sears said, "You know there's more going on here than just two lost boys."

Boggs gave him a steady gaze. "Such as?" Sears took a chair. Again, uninvited. "I was at that bar at the entrance of the park. Hoof and Beer, I think the name is. A spooky damn place with all those glassy eyes staring back at you."

"Hey, now. That's a tourist attraction," Boggs quipped.

Sears answered back, sounding unamused. "For those who still believe they're on the top of the food chain because they own guns." He came to the point. "Walter's father was in the place stirring up customers by telling them Oliver Pitts was found."

Boggs nodded. "He was admitted into the hospital a couple of hours ago."

"Forester was telling them that the Pitts kid told the police Ted Templeton was involved."

Boggs blinked. How had Doug Forester heard all of this in such a short time? Boggs gave a nod. "Ted found Oliver and brought him to the hospital."

"You talk to the kid yet?"

"To Oliver? Yeah." Boggs was undecided whether he'd share what Oliver told him. He didn't appreciate the guy coming into his station, thinking he knew more than him. "I haven't spoken to Ted yet."

This time it was Sears who gave the nod. "You can tell me what the Pitts kid told you later. If I am right, you're going to have your hands full sometime this afternoon. Possibly sooner."

Boggs returned. "What do you mean, hands full?"

"Forester told everyone at that taxidermy eatery he got his information from Chief Moore." Sears paused to let that sink in. He added, "He said the Chief told him more disturbing things were going to be happening."

"Disturbing, like how?" Boggs asked.

Sears shrugged. "I can't say. I'm no mind reader." He smiled. "But I'll tell you what I do think. Forester was suggesting heavily that Ted Templeton killed Jake Cahill. And your police chief may have hinted more kids might turn up dead."

"Drunk talk," Boggs spat. "Chief Moore wouldn't go out of his way to say hello to Forester on the street. And as far as I am aware, he hasn't spoken to Oliver Pitts. I just got back from the hospital. And there is no evidence connecting Ted Templeton to any of this. Ted brought Oliver in for help."

Sears validated his information. "I saw the Chief's car pull out of the parking lot as I pulled in."

A new wrinkle formed on Boggs' brow. "You sure?

Sears nodded. "And one of his men, a skinny guy with a weak chin, was sitting next to me at the bar making friendly. He was dressed like he'd been out fishing, but there was only a faint scent of the lake on him. He didn't smell like fish. I wouldn't have given him much notice, but he started talking to me, chatting me up. It took me a bit to remember him in his uniform. He's been following me."

Boggs fingered a deeply etched wrinkle in his forehead, his fingers following it like the lifeline in the palm of his hand.

"Hayworth," he acknowledged. He thought, if Moore had been to Ed's first, he probably directed Hayworth to go to see what reaction his planted information stirred up.

"Is Forester still there?" Boggs asked.

Sears shook his head. "He got up and left after making his speech. Others followed him out."

Now Boggs was trying to see the scene as Sears described it. Purvis coming in for a private chat with Doug Forester. To what end? To tell him Oliver Pitts had been brought into the hospital by Ted Templeton? To anyone else, that would be a good thing.

But Moore liked to use information for his gain. He bet Moore didn't add the fact it was Ted who found and brought Oliver in.

Boggs made as if to get out of his chair. "I'd better go over to the Forester's. See what Doug Forester is up to." And set him straight, Boggs thought.

"It'd be a shame to waste that roast beef sandwich in the drawer of your desk," Sears said.

Seeing the infuriation darkening Boggs's face, Sears quickly said, "It smells like roast beef. And I'd say it was laced with mustard and onion." Sears opened his hands. *No tricks here.* Jokingly he pulled up his sleeves. *Nothing up my sleeves.* "I smelled it as soon as I came into the office. He paused, said, "Men like Doug Forester aren't hard to figure out. They can be easily manipulated. So, what do you think your Chief of Police has in mind? And for what intent?"

Boggs opened the top drawer of his desk. Reached in and extracted the bagged sandwich. "I take it you haven't had lunch yet?"

Sears shook his head. "Like I said, the place was pretty unappetizing."

"Enough to turn you into a vegetarian?" Boggs asked, a smile hitting his lips.

Sears smiled back. "I'll think about that later." He reached over and took the offered half. "I think we'd better find Ted Templeton before Forester does."

CHAPTER THIRTY-THREE: OFFICER HAYWORTH

Hayworth liked to read crime novels. He knew the first rule to become an undercover cop was being invisible. And believability. A good undercover cop needed to be able to blend in.

Hells bells, Hayworth thought, that Fed had no idea who was sitting beside him. He snickered.

Hayworth had remained a half-mile back on the road as he followed the Fed back into town. Which wasn't difficult. There were few turnoffs. At least none this Fed would find of interest. Not much traffic, either. If the Fed glanced in his rearview mirror, he'd see a police car. Not close. He was not threatening to pull him over.

Heck, the guy could go a hundred miles an hour, and Hayworth wouldn't have pulled him over.

As he drove, Hayworth tried to piece together what he'd learned. But he couldn't put a finger on one thing the Chief might not already know. He hadn't learned where the Fed was from or why he was here. He might have gotten more out of the Fed if Doug Forester hadn't stirred things up.

Hayworth wondered if any of what Forester said would be worth spilling into the Chief's ear. Only, Forester said the Chief came to Ed's specifically to speak with him.

Heck, Hayworth fumed. He'd be in trouble just mentioning to the Chief he'd been in Ed's, sitting right beside the person he was supposed to be stalking, and he hadn't learned a damn thing.

Entering the city limits, Hayworth wasn't surprised at the Fed slowing at City Hall. Or turning into the Sheriff's parking lot.

He wondered what he should do. Should he change back into his uniform and make a surprise visit to the Sheriff's office? Of course, he could tell Boggs he was there to check on how Walter was doing. But wouldn't Boggs wonder why he would come to him when Chief Moore could tell him the same?

Maybe he should go talk to Walter. After all, he was the one who took Walter home. So it wouldn't be out of the question for him to stop by to see how the kid was doing. Now that he thought on it, it was his civic duty.

Yet, he faltered. It may be better to keep low. Wait to see where the Fed went from here.

He turned on the next block onto Main Street, heading in the opposite direction. He parked in a space between two parked cars.

He ducked his head down when he spotted the Chief's car driving down the street. In his direction. If the Chief caught sight of him, he'd want to know why he was parked under a bunch of trees, seemingly off-duty. The Chief would go crazy thinking his orders were being ignored.

Hayworth tried to be careful how far he pushed the Chief's buttons. One time, Hayworth took a break to get a bite of lunch before delivering an envelope to the medical examiner's office. While the Chief said Dr. Potter needed to get the envelope right away, Hayworth didn't think it meant overlooking his lunch hour.

A lesson he didn't need to learn more than once. If the Chief asked him to do something, no matter the time of day, no matter if he'd had a break or not, Hayworth learned to say, "Yes, sir. Right away, sir."

Suddenly there was a knock on the passenger window. Hayworth startled. His mind was on the Chief, and he immediately felt threatened. Instead, he saw a girl, her hands flat on the glass, her face terrified.

"Can you help me," she cried.

Hayworth glanced in his rearview mirror. Where had she come from? There was dirt on her face. Her dark hair appeared tangled as if it hadn't been combed in days. Hayworth guessed she was one of those Hispanic kids who came from the South looking for jobs. She could be illegal, which didn't matter to Hayworth much. People had to do what people had to do to survive. But it would mean paperwork. Lots of paperwork. And if he got side-tracked with her, he couldn't keep an eye on the Fed. Meaning the Chief's foot would be kicking his butt again.

He slowly rolled the window down. "What's wrong, missy?" She looked desperate. "What can I do for you?"

Suddenly, as if she heard something, although Hayworth didn't hear anything, the terror flooding her face was replaced with raw panic.

He glanced in his mirrors, trying to understand the girl's fear. And a little worried about what might be coming at them. The only thing he saw was the Chief's SUV passing City Hall and not turning into the parking lot but continuing to move down the street closer to where he was parked.

When he forced himself to turn back to the side window, she was gone. He spotted her running down the block. He opened his window and leaned out, yelling, "Hey there." He wondered if she'd heard him. She took the corner and continued to run down a side street. He had to admit it, he was relieved.

Hayworth's radio squawked.

"We have a 407 at 1224 Harper's Road. Request assistance."

A 407, unlawful gathering. Hayworth knew the address, the Templeton place. He'd made several calls there when Tira Templeton reported kids bothering the house.

Bunch of spoiled brats, Hayworth told her when she shared how Ted was bullied by neighborhood kids. Hayworth couldn't stomach bullies. He'd been the brunt of teasing himself. A skinny kid, he'd never been popular. Selected last in the PE sports exercises. Stuck with the nerds.

Yet, he did have to admit, there was something a bit weird about Ted Templeton. He was a contradiction in terms. Too smart, some said. Retard, others labeled him. Although, Hayworth had never adopted that word. Some had tried to pin the badge on him. It's why he became a policeman.

He got out of his cruiser and opened the trunk of his car. Behind bushes, he changed back into his uniform. He threw his surveillance clothing in the back seat just in case it was needed again.

Before pulling out from his parking space, he saw Sheriff Boggs rush out of the building into the parking lot. The Fed was right beside him. They got into the Sheriff's SUV.

Hayworth glanced to the street. The SUV had disappeared. He figured the Chief heard the call and was heading in that direction.

He pulled out. If Boggs and the Fed showed up at the Templeton place, he'd better get there before the chief did.

CHAPTER THIRTY-FOUR: CHIEF MOORE

Purvis knew exactly what he would do next, and he knew exactly where to go to take care of the situation.

The bus depot provided a good supply of illegals, who by-passed southern states to come to the mid-west where immigration patrols turned a blinds-eye to those willing to work long hours for little pay. Meat processing plants depended on them.

Carl Hiddleston from the depot called soon after Cletus told him the three girls were missing. He told Moore two girls showed up at his window to purchase tickets for the first bus out. Des Moines. Carl recognized them because he was well acquainted with Pointe House. Even though the one Carl knew well stood a little away from the window, so he might not clearly recognize her, he instantly placed her.

Purvis demanded for Carl to refuse them the tickets. When he heard the tickets were already purchased, and the girls were boarding the bus, his hand touched the butt of his gun with rage.

Now, driving past the bus terminal, he saw it was empty. No buses. Those waiting for the next ride were inside to keep dry and for the air conditioning.

He circled again and again. Each time he seethed. Reminding himself to make sure Carl profoundly understood his error in judgment. Mistakes like this were unforgivable.

On the last circling, he considered going inside. He could check out the pickings to eventually replace the girls should he build another "gentleman's club." But how would he coax a young girl out without creating a stir of curiosity? And where could he hide her?

He couldn't count on Carl. That was for sure.

Better to wait until he had things more under control.

He gripped the steering wheel, his hands growing hard. The numbing in his fists reminded him of the clenched pressure squeezing the girl's throat. The thumping pulse of her heart kept beat with his own.

The thrill of the struggle. Nothing like he had felt before. The thrashing ride she'd given him. His erection hardening as her body kangarooed, attempting to throw him off.

A Brahma bull's rodeo ride. Cinched up tight.

He hungered with need. He shifted in his seat with his discomfort.

He drove away from the depot, turning back toward town. He drove past City Hall, traveling several more blocks until he saw the street he wanted. Risky. But worth the risk.

The high school, middle school, and one of the three elementary schools on Avery Street had been planned in conjunction with one another. City Planning considered the multi-levels a bonus to the city's modernization. The mayor claimed doing so would increase the graduation rates.

Of course, the mayor was also a major developer in the Pinkerton area. And while his company did not oversee the project—a conflict of interest—Purvis knew Mayor Roy Butman dipped his fingers into every area of development.

Not that much went on in his city Purvis didn't know about. Knowledge was a big plus in keeping him Chief for the last fifteen years.

The street was empty of children. The school parking lot spaces barely filled. Then, Purvis remembered that school didn't start until next week. He slammed the heel of his hand on the steering wheel. Where was a kid when you needed one?

He made a quick illegal U-turn in the middle of the street.

He told himself he would go into the office. He still needed to find out why the Fed was in town. Find out what Sheriff Boggs was up to. Get back to the business at hand. He couldn't count on that dimwit Hayworth to come up with anything worthwhile. And Potter? Yeah, he needed to get a handle on Cletus, too.

Cletus had balked on handling the autopsy like he had been told. Maybe he should go by the hospital and have a face-to-face discussion with him. To make sure he understood the seriousness of the situation. The jeopardy he could put them both in.

Then, he spotted her. He was sure she was one of the girls from the house. One of the two girls still missing. What a piece of luck, he thought. This could take care of two things in one.

He slowed the SUV to a crawl.

He couldn't get a good enough view of her. She'd turned, running down a side street out of sight. But it had to be her.

Purvis stopped, giving a wide distance between the SUV and the crosswalk. The street she had taken was Concord Avenue, residential. Single-family homes. Middle-class citizens who couldn't afford one of the larger historical houses in town or have a custom-built on a piece of land at the edge of the city limits. This street was blue-collar. Those who lived on it existed paycheck to paycheck, worked at one of the factories, or drove over to Dayton, an hour away, to work at Walmart.

The risk was high. City Hall was only a block away.

He checked his review mirror. Craned his neck in all directions. He studied the front windows for a shadow—a movement of the curtain.

He gunned his car. Roared down the street, jumping the curb, halting right in front of her. He jumped out. Grabbed her.

"Let me go," she screamed. She clutched his shirt.

He heard something fall to the ground. He put his hand over her mouth before she could scream again. Lifted her and half carried her to the car. If someone did look out their window, they'd see it was him and what appeared to be a Hispanic girl, sixteen, struggling against his arresting her.

She tried to bite him. He gave her a hard fist. She cowered against the seat, trying to get as far away from him as she could. She went for the door handle, but it was locked. She stared at him with her dark eyes, petrified.

"Say another word, and you'll never say another word," Purvis growled.

He searched the windows in the house he was parked in front of. Quiet. Everyone at work. He glanced up and down the street. Nothing stirred.

He couldn't put a name to her face. He never really bothered with their names. Some of them he found hard to pronounce. "Just take it easy," he cautioned. "I'm going to help you."

She spat a glob of spit, hitting his cheek. "Maldito perro. Espero que te vayas al infierno!"

"Fucking bitch," Purvis barked. He wiped the spit from his face.

He thought about pulling out cuffs and restraining her, but he didn't want to take the time. He shut the door and jumped behind the wheel. He'd cuff her as soon as he got out of sight.

"Buckle up, sweetie. We're going for a ride."

CHAPTER THIRTY-FIVE: SHERIFF BOGGS

Boggs unwrapped the sandwich. Gave the second half to Sears.

Sears took a healthy bite. Smiled. "Pretty good." He leaned back in the chair. "I should tell you I did some research on you before coming to Pinkerton."

Boggs chewed. Waited.

"I know you're a methodical investigator. I suspect while your men were looking for those boys, you followed up on the evidence." He grinned, "We're not so different."

Boggs continued eating without reaction. He hated taking the time, feeling he needed to be out there looking for Ted. But he was also hungry. Food and the need to set things right again were fuel to replace his lack of sleep. Plus, Sears was right, the sandwich was good.

"Let's go over what we both know," Sears said. "First, the mutilated deer. How do the gutted deer work with two boys lost in a park?"

Boggs took another taste of his sandwich. He chewed, considering how much he wanted to share. Unfortunately, he still hadn't had a chance to follow up on Sears' authorization. However, if the man could be of help, he would be a fool not to take it.

Ego be damned. He decided to offer what he had heard from both Duel and Riker.

"Bloodless? You're sure?" Sears questioned.

Boggs nodded. "Riker said they looked like they'd been vacuumed clean of it." He paused, asked, "Got any idea what that could mean?"

"No, idea," Sears said.

Sear's eyes stared straight into Boggs', but Boggs noticed the slightest glint of movement, making him suspect that might not be the case. Sear was holding back.

"Second," Sears went on without seeming to need to question further. "What can you tell me about your medical examiner? The girl wasn't killed by the same person that gutted the deer. The girl was murdered. The autopsy showed strangulation. Neck broken. Why was your ME lying?"

Taking the last bite from his sandwich, Boggs thought on how he had never second-guessed Potter's autopsy results in the past.

Again, he considered whether he should continue sharing his opinions with the man sitting across from him. He still wasn't sure why he was in Pinkerton looking for Bill Cahill. He said Cahill contacted him, yet why did Cahill think Sears would make a thousand-mile trip? Or was Sears close by and had contacted Cahill earlier? Good friends? That called for emotional support, not traveling. Colleagues? And why hadn't he come to the police first?

Only Sheriff Boggs. He heard Walter's voice.

If what Walter said was true, and Bill Cahill told his son to tell only Boggs, then why hadn't Cahill come straight to him? Why had he gone to Summit on his own? Or was it he who burned the place down?

Plus, Sears was avoiding Moore. Why?

That question led to a more current issue. Why did Moore go out to the Hoof and Beer to tell Doug Forester about Templeton finding the Pitts kid?

Boggs's mind was whirling with questions without answers. He stopped when he returned to thinking about the autopsy again and how Sears claimed the girl was murdered. He reached over, taking a paper from a file on his desk. He handed it to Sears.

Sears took it and glanced down the page. "Accidental?" He stared over at Boggs. "What the hell is going on? I am telling you that girl was murdered. Another autopsy needs to be done. From an independent ME." Sears added, "Before someone else turns up dead."

"Sheriff?"

Officer Mespelt poked his head in the doorway. "A 407 was called in at 1224 Harper's Road. The Templeton place. I thought you'd want to know."

"Ted Templeton?" Sears asked.

Boggs nodded, got up. "I am going to have to...

Sears interjected. "I'm going with you."

Boggs hesitated. But he knew if he didn't take Sears, the guy would find another way of getting there. He decided it was better to have him close where he could keep an eye on him.

"Okay. But on the way over, I have some questions. And I want answers."

CHAPTER THIRTY-SIX

Boggs pulled out of the parking lot.

As he drove through town toward Highway 99, he continued the conversation from the office, asking Noah if he had gone up to the crime scene again.

Sears nodded.

"Figured you would," Boggs said. "You'd want to see it on your own."

"I hiked from the lake side." He paused, then said, "I met an interesting guy on the way up. He introduced himself as the son of Max."

"Chatan." Boggs made the turn onto the highway. "He probably told you he's Lakota."

"He did," Noah said.

"To tell you the truth," Boggs said, "I can't tell you if he is or isn't. His father, Max Lamott, claimed to be part Lakota." Boggs chuckled. "You would have liked ol'Max. The man had flavor. He used to hang around Ed's telling tales to get a drink. Colorful old guy. His son Chatan lives up somewhere in Eagles. Camps out here and there. Other than his attachment to marijuana, he's harmless. I'm not sure who his mother was. Haven't quite put that story together. Did he say he'd seen the boys?"

Boggs turned off the highway onto a gravel road.

"He didn't say whether he had or hadn't."

"Yep, sounds like Chatan. He speaks his own language. Guess that comes from living isolated."

"I asked him about the house. And Bill Cahill."

"And?"

Sears shrugged. "Like you said, he seems to have his own way of talking. He told me his father was killed, and he prophesied he'd be killed, too."

Boggs thought back to Max's disappearance and reminded himself how no body was discovered. Max disappeared, and he was presumed dead.

He told Sears, "Max's signature cap and a bottle of Thunderbird were found at the lake's dock. No body. And Max never showed up again. The only conclusion we could come to was that he got so drunk and fell off into the lake and drowned. Underground roots may have caught his body. Of course, we had divers search, but Eagles lake is sixty-six acres. Unless a body floats, there is no way to search the entire lake. Someday, something will loosen what's left, and the mystery will be solved.

"I asked the guy who was out to kill him," Sears said.

Boggs looked to Sears, "Did he say who?"

"He said by those who don't like what's different." Sears added, "Right after, he said what is different is really more of the same."

"That sounds like him. He talks in riddles." Boggs stopped. Cars were parked along the road before the turn of the drive. Lights whirled from police cruisers that had taken the call. A house showed on a slight rise. Moderate with a large porch, once painted white with possibly bright green shutters. Now, it appeared shadowed, tired.

"Is this your jurisdiction?" Sears inquired.

"City's," Boggs responded.

Front and center, standing on a wide porch, Boggs recognized the figure of Doug Forester. A crowd again stood below him.

Boggs and Sears walked up the drive. They stayed back from the crowd. This was not his call. Boggs was here to talk to Ted.

"Ask Chief Moore," Forester shouted. He looked around to those standing, listening to him.

Looking for the Chief? Boggs glanced at the crowd. Officers stood outside a group circle, their heads glued to what Forester was saying.

"He'll tell you. The Pitts kid said it was Templeton."

"Come on." Boggs tugged at Sears' arm. "Let's go around back."

They walked wide of the crowd and took a small, weedy path to a back porch, crooked from years and rot. Boggs pulled open the wooden screen door. He knocked.

A voice responded. "Go away..."

"Sheriff Boggs," Boggs said quietly.

The checkered curtains obscuring the view moved. A few seconds later, Tira Templeton opened the door.

"Roger."

"Sorry about all this trouble, Tira. The officers will disperse these men and get them off your property."

"When?" Tira asked. "They've been out there for more than an hour."

Boggs wondered what was keeping Moore. And why the officers weren't dispersing the crowd. Were his men waiting for Moore? Boggs didn't catch the sight of Officer Rants, acting Commander and second in charge. If Boggs had been held up with a call, Deputy Standwick would have immediately taken the lead and handled the situation.

But then, this was Moore. He liked to keep in the center of things. Keep control. He'd once told Boggs being seen by the public reminded them why they needed him.

"I'm sure Chief Moore will be along. If he's not by the time I leave, I'll radio in and let him know the situation."

Moore would love that, Boggs thought. If there was a way to piss off that man's day, it was by calling to tell him he wasn't doing his job.

"I need to talk to Ted," Boggs told her. "Seeing the situation you have here, it might be good if I took him to my office."

Tears sprang in her eyes. "Teddy's not home. I haven't seen him for days."

The tears traveled a path down cheeks already stained.

CHAPTER THIRTY-SEVEN: JACK CAHILL

They all sat before the fire.

Jake was ready to get up and run if he could just figure out how to avoid Teddy's ability to stop him. And he still wasn't buying that there was nothing to fear from IT.

"I need to tell you about Johnny and me. You should know before we leave," Teddy said to Jake.

DONNNNADADDDO

A spark of something glimmered inside ITS cold, dark eyes as it returned Teddy's glance. Emotion? Did IT know what leaving meant?

"When I found Johnny," Teddy began, "my mother told me the story of our birth. She told me about coming to Eagles for a walk. The day had been sunny and bright, and she'd been looking forward to the walk, maybe even a swim. It was summer. About this same time of year. Hot. But, as she walked, she said clouds came in from where there hadn't been clouds, and with them came something else. She said the next thing she knew, she was back home. And later, she found she was going to have a baby." He smiled at Johnny. He corrected himself, "Babies. Us."

Another zing pierced the middle of Jake's forehead. He felt a throbbing as if there was something beneath the skin.

Teddy's voice became shallow, breathless. Was he experiencing the same? Jake looked over to the girl next to Teddy. Her eyes were staring into the fire.

Teddy went on. "My mom remembered more after a time. She said what happened to her wasn't revealed all at once but came in flashes of memory. Like a puzzle waiting for her to put the pieces together. And she didn't tell me all of it at once. But, over time." He took a breath, almost a sigh, "I think she was still trying to understand what happened to her." He glanced at all of us. "When something happens out of the ordinary, it takes a while to stop being frightened by it. You know?"

Jake nodded. He did. Some memory comes back as a blur—a flash without distinction. But, if you concentrate, try to experience it as a now instead of a then, one moment at a time, the past changes to present. And the fear of what happened dissipates.

Sometimes, right before sleep, he called up such memories. And sometimes he could see them as if time hadn't passed. His mother in her kitchen making dinner. He, sneaking around her to nab a bite to eat only to receive a playful whack of her spoon. Or his Dad, coming into the house after being gone for a long time. His father would leave for months without the ability to disclose where he'd gone or when he'd be back. Jake hated those times.

If he couldn't remember the moments exactly, he'd fill in what he wished to remember. His Dad playing catch with him out in the yard. Reading him a story at night before bed. Seeing his dad go into the kitchen, putting his arms around his mother while she made dinner. He, too, would sneak a taste. But she never challenged him with her spoon. Instead, she would turn and put her arms around him, begging him not to leave again. And, he would promise her, *NEVER*.

The more Jake played the game, the more he wasn't sure which memories were real or if the storytelling part of him added images to fill in the spaces.

Was that also the case with the story Teddy was telling? And the story his mother told him?

Teddy continued, breaking into his thoughts. "My mother remembered she saw a funnel of light coming out of the clouds that day she took a walk. Another time, she said she thought she'd been lifted off the ground by the light. She remembered being so far up she could see each end of the lake." Teddy grinned.

"She said she'd thought she'd died and was being lifted up into heaven."

His expression suddenly turned serious. "She also told me about the day we were born. She called your dad, Jake."

"My dad?" Jake was surprised to hear his father mentioned.

Teddy nodded. "She said he was someone she could trust. Someone we could always trust. He came and took her to Dr. Nelson's house."

"You mean the hospital," Jake corrected.

"No, his house. She was specific on that. She gave birth to me." He looked over at IT. "And to Johnny."

Then, he said, but not in an angry way, "Your Dad left my mom with Dr. Nelson, and he took Johnny with him."

My Dad did all of this? When? Seventeen years ago? Dr. Nelson didn't even live in Pinkerton anymore. How could his Dad have kept a secret like this for so long? Jake wondered if his mother knew.

"Okay, let me try to understand this." Jake rubbed his forehead, trying to pale the throbbing so he could wrap a clear mind around what he was being told. "Do both of you have the same kind of illness? And my Dad took your brother to..." He wasn't sure where. "The hospital? Another doctor?"

"No, here," Teddy said.

"Here? Since he was a baby? No way. My Dad would never have done that. Who took care of Johnny? Who fed him? Made sure he was okay?"

"I guess your Dad did, at first. Your dad told my mom Johnny had died. But your Dad helped him hide from people who wouldn't have accepted him. They've never accepted me, so how would they have accepted Johnny?"

Again, another rumble of thunder exploded.

Jake was still trying to tie his Dad with all of this...IT...him, Johnny. He shook his head, telling himself as well as Teddy, "He was gone a lot. He couldn't have done what you're saying."

"Others helped," Teddy said. But I don't know about them. Storms come and go. I think Max Lamott helped. And Max's son."

Jake baited, "Why didn't your mom take him back home when you told her you found him? Why leave him here?"

"I didn't tell her about Johnny until this last big storm. Your Dad told me not to. He said it was too dangerous. And we would be leaving, Johnny and I." He said to Jake, "I need you to tell my mom that we are okay. That we WILL be okay."

Another ice-piercing spark pinged Jake's head. The throbbing in his forehead grew until there wasn't space between his thoughts. He could hear a pulsating tone inside his mind, in his ears, like a dull bell being rung.

Again, he looked at Johnny.

His Dad knew? Jake recalled how his Dad would come to Eagles every time he was in town. To hike, he said. To go fishing. And he wouldn't always bring Jake, no matter how much Jake begged. Sometimes, when his Dad's friends visited, they went with him.

Jake looked over to the girl. She'd been quiet through Teddy's story. Jake asked her, "You said my dad saved you?"

She nodded but kept her eyes to the fire. "Men held us captive in the house."

"But not my Dad? He wouldn't have done that."

"No, other men," the girl said. "One a policeman." Still, she kept her gaze to the fire, as if wishing to tell but not remember. "They did terrible things to us. When your Dad came to the house, he saw me. And I thought it might be my only chance to escape. I saw it in your dad's face. He would help me. I cried out. I told him we were being held captive. That the man was hurting us.

"And I ran to him. He and the man who said he was a policeman, who said he would protect us but only did horrible things to us, who beat us, raped us, they got into a fight. My friends, other girls, came down and they saw the fighting. We all ran. We all got away, but...

She burst into sobs.

Jake had never been prouder of his father. He turned to Teddy. "I still don't understand why my Dad hid your brother." This time he made sure he didn't say IT. His father had taken care of him. And Jake didn't want his father ever to think he was like the other men that Teddy feared.

"We do not have an illness," Teddy said. "Just because you're different, look different, speak different, doesn't mean you are different. Not truly. It doesn't mean you don't belong.

"I'm not sick, Jake. Your Dad knew why we look the way we do. He understood. And we are not so different. There are many like us, but they look normal. Like Max." Teddy smiled. "Max Lamott once said to me that there was nothing wrong with me, and one day, everyone would understand that we are all the same."

Jake remembered Max once saying how people thought they had a leg up, but how everyone stood on legs. And those that had no legs, they moved around in the same space, breathed in the same air, wanted to live as much as the next guy.

Jake reflected on when he and his father had been lying outside, looking up into the stars. There were so many. A Ka-trillion universes. As they lay looking up, Jake thought how there was so much that wasn't known. His dad knew a little, but he even said there was more he didn't know. And he'd been in orbit. He'd told Jake when he first saw the earth, he realized how small it was. Like he could almost hold it in his hand, compared to the vast darkness of the unknown.

Jake had told his Dad he hoped to see that one day. And his dad said he was sure Jake would.

Jake's memory stayed on that night, he and his dad, remembering how the stars seemed to fall toward the Earth as he felt like he was moving further into space. He asked his dad if he could feel it, too. Almost a feeling of falling into, instead of up. His dad said there was no real separation between any and all of it. It was all one.

"I saw my father in the hospital," Jake told Ted. "He could hardly talk, but he whispered the words Eagles Nest. I thought he meant I would find my mom and sister up here at Eagles. I thought he'd found them."

He asked the girl, "My mom and sister weren't with you guys, were they?"

She shook her head no.

He looked to Teddy. "Is my father dead?"

CHAPTER THIRTY-EIGHT: MAJOR SEARS

The room was a small kitchen.

Tiled counters shined clean but crowded with cookbooks, a large mixer, a stack of baking pans, and mail that appeared to have been left unopened for several days. Rag rugs covered a clean linoleum flooring. To some, the room may have been seemed old and cluttered, but Sears had a feeling Ted's mother knew where everything was and ready for a finger's touch.

"You know he likes to be out," she was telling Boggs as Sears stepped into the living room.

This room was crowded with furniture. Old, well-oiled antiques probably handed down through the family placed next to more modern chairs. A sofa with a slumping center from years of use.

The woman had followed him into the room. Tira Templeton stood short and round next to Boggs' husky, tall stature. Her eyes blinked red and swollen from the lack of sleep.

"He's been in and out more than normal since the storm. He knows not to worry me." She added as if her statement needed further explanation. "He's seventeen. He's not a little boy anymore." She wiped new tears off her face with the back of her hand. Sniffed. "I'm afraid for him, Roger. "He's...." Raised voices from outside stopped her.

Sears stepped over to the window and looked out. Forester was madly waving his arms. Those listening were shrugging theirs, twisting shoulders with a want to move, raising their voices to be heard above the person standing next to them.

When he turned back to the room, he found Tira Templeton staring at him. "Have we met before?" she asked.

Sears shook his head. "I'm a friend of Bill Cahill's. I became involved in all of this because his son's missing."

"Bill," she said wistfully. "I wish he were here. He'd know what to do." She took her notice away from Sears and back to Boggs, saying, "They think Teddy had something to do with the boys, don't they?"

Boggs gave a nod. "But Oliver Pitts has been found."

"Thank God. Is he okay?"

"He's fine."

"Then you've seen Teddy?"

"I saw him for just a moment standing outside of the hospital. It was Ted who found Oliver and carried him to the hospital." Another shout came from outside. Boggs said, "I need to find Ted. He may be able to lead us to where he found Oliver so that we can find Jake Cahill."

All three heard a chorus of shouting, "Let's go!"

Sears said to Boggs, "I think we've got trouble out there."

Boggs immediately went over to the front door. He stuck his head back in, looking at Sears, "You coming?"

Sears turned to Tira, then back to Boggs. "I'll stay here in case Ted shows up, or those guys get it in their heads to bombard the house."

Boggs paused, but the sound of a gunshot took him out the door. Sears hurried to the window.

He saw the officer who had sat behind him at Ed's Hoof and Beer holding his gun high in the air. His face appeared stunned, as shocked as if it had been someone else who had pulled the trigger.

CHAPTER THIRTY-NINE: OFFICER HAYWORTH

"Forester," Boggs shouted.

"This is over. All of you. Get in your cars and go home. None of what you're hearing is true. I spoke to Oliver Pitts a little while ago. He's unhurt. He said Ted Templeton found him and brought him to the hospital." He turned and zeroed his gaze straight at Forester. "He had nothing to do with the boys missing."

Hayworth didn't know what to do. He looked to his fellow officers for some clue what the next step should be. He stretched further up on his toes, gawking over heads, trying to find Chief Moore. Hayworth wondered why Sheriff Boggs was on the porch dismissing the crowd and not the Chief.

Forester shouted back, "Didn't you hear, Sheriff? They've found another dead girl. Ted Templeton is killing our children."

"Let's get'em," Donald Goode standing next to Hayworth, shouted.

"Find Templeton before he kills another kid," Phil Wilmer, a golfing buddy of Goode's, yelled.

"Angels Park. Come on. Let's go." More and more of the men gathered began shouting. Men raced to their vehicles. Forester urging them on.

Hayworth drew his gun. His finger was on the trigger. He continued to glance about, hoping the Chief would show himself. Then, there was a shot. The sound of the blast made him jump. He hadn't realized his finger was holding the trigger so tight. He'd never shot a gun before except in target practice.

Hell's fire, what did he do?

Those running stopped. They turned on their heels, mouths opened in awe.

"Now wait a damn minute," Hayworth shouted. "All of you. Stay where you are. Let the police handle things."

The men, huffing and puffing, their bodies still in motion, had slowed down but had not completely stopped. He glared over at him.

And in that same fluidity, they jerked back around to their cars and trucks. Doors clunked open and slammed shut.

"Where are you, Chief?" Hayworth groaned.

CHAPTER FORTY: MAJOR SEARS

"You don't need to stay," Tira said to Sears.

"I'll wait until everyone's left to make sure there's no further trouble." Sears came over and sat down on the slumping couch.

Tira took a chair near him. Her hands worrying in her lap.

Sears said, "I need you to tell me about Teddy."

"Teddy is a good boy," she said. "He does very well in school. He was just accepted to the University of Iowa. I had to push him a bit to apply. He's been badly bullied and shy around people. But I told him college is different." She paused, thoughtfully, continuing. "Usually, he isn't involved in so much mischief. I don't think he's involved now. Not like they're claiming." Her eyes went to the front window. "Teddy wouldn't hurt anyone. He may be different...but..."

Sears thought, *I need to know Teddy's story.*

Her eyes grew wide. Sears knew she had heard him.

She whispered, "Who are you?"

"Major Noah Sears from a special forces unit with the Federal Government.

Fear bloomed on her. Her eyes went again to the front window. She scooted to the lip of her chair as if ready to run.

Sears raised his hand. "Don't worry. I'm here to help."

"We don't need any help," she stammered.

"Ms. Templeton, I need to find Teddy before the others find him. I need you to tell me about Teddy."

Her eyes moved about the room, still frightened.

He continued to encourage her. "I believe you had an unusual experience. Let me assure you, you aren't the first woman I've met who has had such an experience. Bill told me a little about Teddy. Now, I need you to tell me more."

Her head jerked to him. She stared open-eyed. "There are others?"

"There are many others," Sears assured her.

She quieted in her manner, her body pooling in the chair. She nodded. "I thought so. I think there are others here, too. In Pinkerton. Sometimes I can hear the thoughts of other people. And I am sure they can hear mine. Although, none of us speak of it. It's like a very dark secret everyone thinks will go away if it's never said aloud." She bit her lower lip, said, "They look at Teddy as if he's different than they are. The kids, and even some adults, bully him. It's why I told everyone I took him to a doctor in Iowa City, and that he has a disease."

She halted. Gave herself some time. "He may look different, Major Sears, but not everyone looks the same. He is no different than some others here and around."

Sears encouraged her. "You can trust me."

"Can I? Can Teddy?"

"With his life," Sears said.

At first, she looked again as if she was going to run.

"You can trust me." He held out his hands and leaned across to her.

She took his into her own.

She took a deep breath. "I don't have all the answers to what happened. I'm still so full of questions, even after these seventeen years. If you can help Teddy, then I will tell you. I don't care about keeping myself safe any longer. I'm old. No one wants me. But him? I haven't ever felt he's been safe, from anything. If you can..."

Sears said, "I not only can, but will."

She began. "And then, there is his twin brother."

Sears nodded. Bill had told him about the twin boys born.

"I think Teddy is with his brother Johnny. He told me he had found Johnny. I told him what I could, and then he said Bill told him more about him and his brother. That was right before the storm. And he was going to take me to him, but then the tornado hit. It started happening all over again."

CHAPTER FORTY-ONE: SHERIFF BOGGS

Fiery halos of red and blue filled Concord Street.

Cruisers parked willy-nilly. The entrance was left unbarricaded. An ambulance waited with its back doors held open.

People walked quickly to see what was going on. Others, still in residence, stood outside their houses, calling out to others seeking answers to what was happening.

Boggs parked as best he could to allow for necessary traffic flow. He kept an eye out for Chief Moore's SUV as he walked onto the scene.

He knew Concord Street dead-ended. Drivers were then forced to turn left or right. Straight-on was a drainage ditch that flooded during the winter. And beyond it lay an empty piece of land planned twenty years ago for a public playground. Still to be completed.

Not seeing Moore's vehicle, Boggs thought he could have come in from one of the other streets. Parked closer to the crime scene. And this activity answered why Moore hadn't shown up at the Templeton place.

Boggs found city officers at the end of the street, talking quietly, waiting for instructions. They parted, allowing him through. Acting-Commander Rants came forward—his expression grave. "You may want to pass this one up," he said to Boggs.

"Where's your boss?" Boggs inquired.

Rants shrugged. "Hasn't shown yet. I left Roth and Zelhke down at Main to turn the crowd around. Keep them from trampling everything. Although, I can't say we got here before others took a good look." He shook his head. "Jesus, this poor kid will haunt their dreams for months."

"How old?" Boggs asked.

"Teenager." Rants glanced away and then back. "Whoever did this brutalized this girl." He choked. "Man, I need some air."

Boggs walked to the ditch to see Dr. Potter examining the victim. He saw her t-shirt was covered in blood, half-torn off. Her jeans were thrown carelessly a few feet away. She'd been raped.

Before or after she'd been gutted? Boggs wondered.

The mugginess of the day and seeing this girl emptied the air of breath and clamped a sweaty hand on the back of his neck. Dr. Potter rose from out of the ditch. "We've got to get these people out of here."

"Rants is already on it," Boggs told him. "What can you tell me about her."

Potter wiped his face with his hand. Turned his back to the ditch. His face darkened with anger. "This site's been trashed. I can't tell you how many climbed down here tramping around before I came."

Potters' people were placing the girl into a body bag.

"Cause of death?" Boggs asked.

"Strangled," Potter said. "Before, she was torn open. Raped."

"How long?"

"I'd say not more than an hour, maybe less." Potter moved to allow the gurney through.

"Think it's the same person who killed the girl up on Summit?"

At first, Boggs thought Potter was going to correct him. Tell him, like he had during the autopsy, that the girl had fallen, broken her neck, and then animals got to her. But his eyes wavered. He glanced about. "You seen Moore?"

The crowd was thinning, turned away now by the officers. He saw Officer Zelhke running a yellow plastic barrier from street corner to corner across Concord, then across to the vacant lot.

Officer Ben Strait came up with Officer Hayworth behind him. "Chief just called Hayworth," Strait told him.

"Must have been helping with the search at Eagles," Hayworth said. His hands flapped at his sides as if he wasn't sure where to put them. He stood wide-eyed, looking everywhere but at Boggs. "He's on his way."

Potter seemed unrelieved at the news, growling, "I'm headed to the hospital. He can find me there."

Boggs asked Officer Strait. "You guys got this? Or you need me to wait until the Chief gets here?"

"Rants is in charge until the Chief gets here," Strait assured him. "But let me tell you, this wasn't on my to-do list for today. I've got a kid not much older than this girl." He paused, his voice lowering slightly, "I'd rather be out helping them search."

Why was Moore out at Eagles? Boggs wondered. Did he plan to meet Forester's group out there?

He said to Potter. I want an autopsy done right away. And I want to know if this girl was cut open by the same type of knife used on the girl up at the Summit. He added. "You were wrong, Cletus. And if we don't get a handle on what's going on here, an innocent boy might be the next victim."

CHAPTER FORTY-TWO: OFFICER HAYWORTH

Hayworth was sure of two things. One, he'd seen the Chief's SUV near Concord Street. And two, Concord was in the opposite direction of going out to Highway 99.

Again, he found himself forced to decide. Should he find the Fed and stick to him like the Chief ordered? Or should he figure out where Boggs left off to?

He hefted his duty belt on his hips. Sniffed.

He decided on Eagles. After all, the Chief was on his way back from there. And the Fed had been with Boggs at the Templeton house. Hayworth decided he might find both at the park.

But hold it. There was a third thing bothering him. Wouldn't the Chief have heard the same dispatch he'd heard about the problem out at the Templeton place? Yet, he'd gone out to Eagles instead. Why? Had the Chief found the girl?

Hayworth thought on this as he walked back to the street entrance at Concord and Main, where his cruiser was still parked. He was halfway back when his eye caught a shiny object in the gutter. He went over. Picked it up. It was a metal pin, with two flags. The US flag and the Iowa Flag. The same type of pin the Chief wore.

"Hayworth?"

Hayworth jerked to attention at the sound of his name.

"Where the hell's the Chief?" Rants shouted

"On his way," Hayworth returned, stepping over to him. "I was coming looking for you. I have to head out." Hayworth thought of Rants as one of the good guys. An officer who, like him, took pride in his badge and uniform.

"Didn't Strait tell you?" Hayworth asked.

"Tell me what?" Rants growled.

"Chief Moore called and told me he was headed back in from Eagles."

"Why'd he call you?" Rants demanded.

Hayworth didn't know how to answer that. But he knew how the others talked about him behind his back. Mocked him. Said how he was like the Chief's dog. Constantly being told to fetch.

But telling Rants that the Chief was coming back didn't make sense if it was the Chief who found the dead girl.

Rants cursed, "Why the hell hasn't he been answering dispatch."

Hayworth shrugged. "Just called and told me he was headed here."

"How long ago?"

"Twenty minutes?" Hayworth offered. Although, he thought it could have been longer. He didn't like Rants putting him on the spot. He added, "Or about there."

Should he tell Rants about seeing the Chief driving onto Concord? Could the Chief have witnessed the guy attacking the girl and took off after him? But again, that didn't make sense. The Chief said he was out at Eagles. And if he was in pursuit, and the pursuit took him out by Eagles, why wouldn't he have called for backup?

Hells- bells, Hayworth's mind raced. He grabbed hold of his duty belt. Not to hoist it to his hips, but as something to hang on to. His apprehension shook him from his head to his knees.

He looked Rants square in the eyes. "You'll have to take his timing up with him when he gets here."

Rants blew out a puff of air in exasperation. Turned away and then back as if calculating a reply. Rants said, "I need you to help keep this place cleared out while I get men to start knocking on doors."

"I've got my orders," Hayworth stated. "Now that the Chief's on his way, he'll be wanting me to get back to it."

Back in his cruiser, Hayworth breathed a sigh of relief. Not for having dared to refuse Rants, but for having decided what to do in his mind. He continued to sit, listening to his radio bark the voices from dispatch to officers, and he heard Rants on the radio demanding to know where Chief Moore was and his ETA.

Hayworth felt the bulge in his pocket. The Chief had been here on this street about the same time the girl was murdered. But then, why was the Chief calling him to tell him he was coming in from Eagles? And why didn't the Chief show up at the Templeton place?

Hells-bells!

CHAPTER FORTY-THREE: SHERIFF BOGGS

Boggs grabbed the radio.

"Standwick. Keep an eye out. Doug Forester's rallied a gang of do-gooders, and they're headed your way hell-bent on finding Ted Templeton."

"Some are already here," Standwick radioed back. "I haven't seen Forester yet, but his so-called friends are headed up Summit Trail. I've got to tell you, I'm worried things might get out of hand. Many of them are armed."

"God damn that Forester," Boggs roared. "Get that pitch-fork gang out of there. And if you see Forester, arrest him."

"On what charge?"

"Inciting a riot for one," Boggs ordered. "Let's hope we don't have to add attempted murder. I will be there in ten. I'm turning onto 99 as we speak." He added, "And Standwick, if you see Sears, keep him with you until I get there."

CHAPTER FORTY-FOUR: CHIEF MOORE

Purvis parked his SUV in his garage.

He sat quietly, trying to lessen the frantic beat of his heart. The surge of terror.

He needed to get out of Pinkerton. Hell, leave Iowa. Maybe the country.

He entered the house. Empty. Headed to his study. A room where he secluded himself every night shortly after dinner. *To catch up on paperwork.*

"He's a workaholic," his wife Nancy told others.

His study was his, and his alone. Nancy and the kids knew better than interrupt him there.

He went over to his computer and deleted the online history. Forensics could recover files. They would eventually find the blackmail records. The photos. But why make it easy for them? Of course, they'd interrogate Nancy. But she hadn't a clue what was going on.

Or did she know more than she let on? Purvis paused a moment to think about that. Where the hell did she think he got the extra money she lavished on herself? She would probably have to move. People would shun her. His children would suffer.

He'd never touched either of his daughters. He'd have killed anyone who even thought of putting their hands on them. But... would they remember their daddy as the man who gave them piggy-back rides, or tickled them, their pealing laughter begging him to stop? Or would they remember only the man others said raped and held captive defenseless girls?

He shoved his desk back and pulled up the carpeting. Knowing this day would eventually arrive—*don't all good things eventually come to an end*—he'd hinged floorboards beneath his heavy desk to create a safe place. Opened now, he grabbed ahold of the sack containing a faked passport, ten thousand dollars in cash, and the keys to a 1980 Honda Civic he stored on the other side of town.

He kept the same type of stash at Pointe House. Just in case. One evening while he and Cletus sipped a whiskey, satiated from their entertainment, and waiting for the AirCare, they'd discussed how all good things eventually might come to an end. Purvis told Cletus he was ready. In fact, he saw it all as a Butch Cassidy and Sundance Kid kind of moment. He'd grab the stash he kept, and he'd make a run for it.

Potter, the coward, laughed. He said he was getting out before that happened. He said he thought it was time for them to close operations down and sell the house before things got too messy. Give the girls a one-way ticket to where they would like to go. A little cash to get them by. Destroy all the evidence.

Purvis now grinned. The evidence was destroyed. He had Cahill to thank for that.

Adrenaline surged through his body, swelling his gist for the win. Nothing would stop him, he thought. Expect, Potter. A loose end he needed to take care of before leaving. Potter would rat him out for a plea. He was still pissed at him about having killed his piece of ass. Potter was a liability.

He disrobed and shoved his uniform into the floorboards. Not only could Potter finger him, but he hadn't been thinking when he killed this last one. His DNA was all over that girl.

Damn that Jeannie Calloway. If she hadn't come outside calling for her kid...he was sure she saw him. Probably saw his SUV parked. And once the body was found?

A voice whispered as he pushed the desk back into place:

Cover your ears Purvie when you hear the bad angel whispering to steal money out of my purse. Don't take things that aren't yours. God wants you to be a good boy.

His mother held the leather belt she'd lifted off the peg in the kitchen. It hung like an ornament as a reminder of God's word.

His mother's voice haunted him beyond her own grave. Even when he pinned on the badge as Chief of Police, he'd heard her: Never will amount to anything. She whispered: Devil eats bad boys for lunch. Devil's waiting for you.

His attention jerked back to where he was standing, naked.

What was that? He glanced at his watch. But Nancy wouldn't be home yet. And he knew the kids were over at her sister's.

Waiting for you...

"Shut the fuck up," Purvis demanded.

Then he heard Nancy's voice.

She was in the house. What was she doing home so early?

He hurried over to a window and peered out. Her new Caddie was parked in the drive. She never left the car parked outside. Not if she was going to be home for long.

He worked his way across the room, watching where he stepped, missing those places where the floorboards creaked. He opened the study door an inch. Listened.

She was in the kitchen. "I haven't spoken to Purvis yet, but you can bet he won't sleep until he's caught this pervert."

A girl at Pointe House once called him a pervert. The next time he was with her, she decided the black and bruising he gave her wasn't worth her unwanted opinion.

He heard the refrigerator open and close. Her high-heels clicked on the tiles. *Clip, clip.* A cupboard latching. Then the sound of keys. *Clip, clip, clip.* The sound of the front door closing.

He waited until he heard the revving of the Caddie before slipping out from the study and racing to the bedroom. He pulled on jeans and a shirt. Found his hooded sweatshirt in the dirty clothes, smelling of the acrid sweat from his last workout. He tugged it on.

Shoving his security bag and some other clothes into his gym bag, he left through a door to the backyard. Gave a quick glance around before running across the yard, crawling over the back fence, heading to the storage garage for the out-of-state licensed Civic.

CHAPTER FORTY-FIVE: SHERIFF BOGGS

Standwick must have been watching for him because he was at the SUV's door as soon as Boggs stepped out.

"Forester's carrying a rifle. We've talked some of the guys into giving up the manhunt." He reported, "We took Donald Goode to the hospital. Someone shot him in the leg."

Boggs knew he needed to get this stopped before any more were hurt. He asked, "Has Sears shown up?"

Standwick said, "I think you might want to call Deputy Warner. She took off for her office before you called, saying she had some information come in and would be back."

Boggs nodded. He went over to his SUV. He had dispatch connect him with the park's deputy station.

"I'm glad Standwick told you to call me," Warner said. Her voice was measured as if she'd already formulated the information she'd received and was ready to pass it on. "I put some feelers out about that house. Old-timers in the area told me it was originally used as a private hunting club back in the day. Built and owned by a Stover Powell. You've probably heard the name."

"Any relation to Norman Powell of Powell Electrics?" Boggs glanced to the trail, not knowing where this information was going and more than anxious to get started on up to stop Forester.

"Shirt-tail relation at this point in history," Warner returned. "This was way back. About seventy-five or more years. The old-timers were surprised the place was still standing. Kenny

Minor said he thought the place burned down a long time ago and was left to rot."

"Sure it's the same place?"

"I called up County Planning and started trying to follow the deeds of trust. Not an easy task, I'll tell you. CP isn't well organized when looking for paperwork that far back. Not all of it's on the computer.

"Someone named Mentzer bought the property about twenty years ago. And I think you'll find this interesting." She paused as if giving him time to catch up with all she'd told him. "He sold the house to Cletus Potter."

"Can you repeat that, Elizabeth? I think I heard you wrong."

"Cletus Potter," she repeated. "And no, you didn't hear me wrong. I haven't been able to get my head around it either."

Boggs remembered Potter saying he hadn't known about the place. *Used by those who come across it. Clearly, whoever was last in it wasn't being careful."*

CHAPTER FORTY-SIX: CHIEF MOORE

Purvis pulled the Honda Civic into Pinkerton General Hospital's parking lot.

He glanced around, then pulled the hood of his sweatshirt over his head. He wasn't sure where he would find Potter, but he had to find him, and fast.

He took the stairs to the second floor, where Potter kept an office. It was empty. He then decided to head to the autopsy room. Potter may have been pressured to start in on the girl.

Before he could get back to the stairway, he heard his name. "Chief Moore? Is that you?"

He saw Liz Torres give a wave. She headed towards him.

He had no choice but to wait. If he ignored her, she would still remember seeing someone who looked like him in the hospital. When he was supposed to be headed to the crime scene.

"I wasn't expecting to see you. I just checked on Phil Wilmer. He's okay."

He had no idea what she was talking about. But, he replied, "Thanks."

"Shot by Donald Goode. Weird, huh? They being best friends and all."

He had no time for this woman. And why Goode may have shot Wilmer was interesting, but not so much to risk his chance of getting out of Pinkerton as soon as possible. "I'm looking for Dr. Potter."

"I'm sure you want to talk to him about that poor girl. What's Pinkerton coming to, Chief Moore? Men we know, good men like Donald Goode, half-crazed out of their minds taking the law into their own hands? A girl raped and killed."

"Is Dr. Potter with Wilmer?"

She shook her head. "I heard one of the nurses say he needed to leave the hospital for a few minutes." Then she seemed to notice he was out of uniform. She studied him, her face puzzled.

Purvis didn't wait for her question. "I was out for a jog when I got the call about the girl," he told her. "I've got to get back to the office."

He turned as if to go to the stairs but thought better of it. Instead, he made his way to the elevator.

He was relieved to find the nurses' desk vacant, and no more distractions and meaningless questions. The elevator opened at the push of the button.

Back at the Civic, he felt reasonably sure he'd gotten by without being noticed by anyone else. And he could fathom no reason for Liz Torres to mention him. Not yet, anyway.

He turned out of the hospital's parking lot and headed toward Potter's house.

CHAPTER FORTY-SEVEN: OFFICER HAYWORTH

Officer Hayworth took his foot off the gas, seeing Sheriff Boggs' SUV, at high speed, traveling by from the opposite direction, away from Eagles Park.

He caught a glimpse of Boggs' face. His eyes stared straight ahead, intent on where he was going, and didn't glance over to Hayworth's cruiser.

And Hayworth noted, he was alone. The Fed wasn't with him.

Hayworth continued watching the SUV through his rearview, wondering why the Sheriff was heading back into town and at the speed he was traveling. Warning lights off.

He became even more concerned when he saw the SUV turn a corner onto a street leading to Pinkerton General. His first thought was of the Chief missing.

He was at the entrance to Highway 99. He continued staring at the road behind him. Should he continue to Eagles? Or turn around?

He got on the radio, thinking he would check with dispatch to see if the Chief made it to the crime scene. If so, that would tell him Boggs came back into town for something else. Maybe Forester's men got hold of Ted Templeton. Had they hurt him?

He learned from dispatch that Acting-Commander Rants was half out of his mind demanding to know where Chief Moore was. Dispatch asked if Hayworth had heard any further from him. The woman on the other end of the radio sounded a bit frantic with having so many people asking her, and she, unable to direct them.

That was where Sheriff Boggs must be heading, Hayworth decided. Something had happened to the Chief.

He made an immediate illegal U-turn. Fire d up his lights.

But by the time, he reached the parking lot of Pinkerton General, Boggs' SUV was racing out of the lot. Lights now burning.

FORTY-EIGHT: CHIEF MOORE

Purvis parked the Civic down the block away from Potter's two-story Colonial-styled home.

The house made the local papers when his wife was alive. *Garden Club President Mrs. Cletus Potter Wins Most Beautiful Garden of the Year. Historical Colonial held as Pinkerton Historical Society's Pride of Ownership Winner*. Today, the chimney on the house appeared crooked, knocked off-center from the tornado's winds ravaging through the neighborhoods.

Purvis kept to the side of the front yard where overgrown shrubs hid his view from the street. The side gate leading into the backyard stood off its latch. He knew Potter kept a study on the ground floor.

The drapes in the study were drawn. A small slit where they lacked gathering in the middle allowed him to see inside. The lights were off. The room appeared empty.

Going to the garage, Purvis rubbed the dusty-covered windowpanes clean to get a better look inside. Martha's Buick parked near the window had an old quilt draped over it. One she probably made, Purvis thought. She had been known for her quilting as well as the garden.

"Why hadn't Cletus got rid of the car?" Purvis wondered. She'd been dead for more than five years. He'd never seen Cletus driving it. And a car not driven, Purvis's father always said, was like a virgin languishing for the seed of life.

Cletus' Lincoln Navigator stood parked on the other side of the Buick.

He was home.

Purvis headed back to the house and around to the front. He tried the front door and found it locked. Then, going to the back door, he pulled his gun from where he'd tucked it into his waistband. He took off his sweatshirt. Wrapping the butt of the gun in the soft material, he gave the window glass a crack. Broken glass clattered to the floor.

Purvis reached in. Turned the deadbolt.

Listened.

Kitchen counters appeared bare of living. Purvis pushed the swinging door open slowly to view the dining room. A large mahogany table set in the middle of the room with a crystal chandelier hanging over its center. The room smelled of dust. The drapes in this room were drawn as well.

But Cletus had to be here, Moore thought. Where else could he be?

Then, something dropped on the floor upstairs directly above him.

Purvis hurried quietly around to the entry, and he was just about to climb the stairs when Potter appeared carrying two suitcases.

Purvis pulled back into the shadows.

Half-stumbling from the weight in the heavy bags, Potter continued coming down.

Definitely not going for an overnight, Purvis thought.

When he'd stepped off the last step, Purvis surprised him. "Taking off on vacation, Cletus?"

Cletus's head jerked toward the voice. His eyes widened in seeing not only Purvis but the gun aimed at him.

He took a breath and steeled a look at Purvis. "I've been party to this madness for too long. Be aware, Purvis, I know it was you who killed the girl today."

"She was no different from some of the girls you've poked and prodded." Purvis sneered, "You think your shit doesn't stink. But remember, you didn't try to stop me from killing that girl up at the house. Oh, you screamed and whimpered, but you did nothing to save her."

Potter moaned, "My sweet Josie."

"Purvis chuckled. "Did you really think she cared about you?"

"We planned to..." Cletus glanced beyond Purvis.

"Good God, she would have run the first chance she got. She'd have probably stuck a knife in your belly as a thank you."

Potter's eyes narrowed. "You're sick, Purvis."

"A doctor should know." Purvis laughed. "So what's your advice? Got a prescription to cure this?"

"Give up." Potter sighed deeply. "I'm ready to turn myself in."

Purvis pointed the gun toward the suitcases. "I don't think you'll be moving into any Hilton when they put bracelets around your wrists."

Cletus took a step away from the suitcases, moving closer to the door.

"Stay where you are," Purvis warned.

"I can't do this." He then gave Purvis a sideways glance. "Let's go out like we talked about, like Butch Cassidy and the Sundance Kid."

Drunken bullshit. Purvis had no desire to replay the fictional scene. "If you remember, Butch and Sundance were both killed. I have some living yet to do."

"You won't get away with this." Cletus grinned wickedly. "You're not so perfect, Purvis? Not infallible like you want others to think. Let me tell you the truth while I still can. You were never perfect. You've made mistakes."

Purvis aimed the gun at Cletus's head. His finger itched. This little chit-chat was taking time he didn't have. "Final last words?"

"Hurry up and get it over with," Cletus demanded.

A loud banging came from the front door.

CHAPTER FORTY-NINE: SHERIFF BOGGS

Boggs parked on the street in front of Potter's house and strode quickly to the front door.

He knocked. No answer. But he heard voices.

He knocked again, this time harder. Not to be ignored, "Potter, we need to talk."

Moments went by. The voices quieted. Then the door opened.

Cletus Potter stood with his head pointing towards Boggs, but his eyes were fixed to the side as if he were trying to look over his own shoulder. He appeared pale. Worry lines deepened in his face. His mouth curved downward, and the muscles in his cheek twitched.

Boggs' first thought was that Potter knew why he was here. But that thought was quickly dismissed. There had been two voices he heard, and if he wasn't mistaken, the other voice sounded like Moore's. Only, Moore's SUV wasn't on the street.

Who was inside? Boggs wondered. Whoever it was made Potter anxious.

"Deputy Warner contacted me." Boggs kept his guard up for anything unexpected. Potter kept bringing his eyes to him and then quickly looking back as if trying to see over his shoulder. As if asking Boggs to take a look."Warner found ownership of that house on Summit. It turns out it's titled in your name."

Boggs expected Potter to answer in the negative. Tell him he'd gotten the information wrong. That Warner's facts were erroneous. Instead, Potter did the unexpected. He smiled. And keeping the smile, he turned his eyes from Boggs again back to over his shoulder.

Was there also a slight nod of his head?

"Can I come in, Cletus?" Boggs asked, trying to see around Potter.

"I'm just getting ready to go out," Potter returned, his body shifting slightly as if to give Boggs a clearer viewpoint.

Suddenly, Potter's body jumped as if he'd been jolted. His eyes huge. Pleading?

Boggs tried to assess the situation. Who was inside? And why was Potter frightened?

"I won't be but a minute," Boggs quickly argued. "I just want to get a few facts straight." He took a step towards Potter. And as he did, Potter moved as if to let him in.

Boggs saw Moore, and the gun.

"Now, isn't this a pickle?" Moore said.

"What the hell's going on?" Boggs demanded.

Moore was dressed as if off duty. "Put that damn gun away, Purvis. Have you lost your mind?"

Potter remained in the open doorway. Boggs noticed how he'd moved only enough to give Boggs space to get in. Was the man thinking of making a run for it?

"Not a good idea, Cletus," Moore saw the same. "Shut the door so that we can have a private conversation."

Potter hesitated. He seemed to consider his chances, but thought better of it and shut the door.

Moore waved his hand for Potter to move away from the door.

"What's this all about, Purvis?" Boggs demanded.

Stymied, he looked to Potter for answers. "What the hell's going on here?"

"Why don't the two of you move into the dining room," Moore suggested. "We can sit down and sort this little problem out." He took a step back, allowing room for both to pass in front of him.

"I'm not going anywhere," Potter said. "If you're going to shoot me, Purvis, get it over with. I'm not playing your game any longer." He said to Boggs, "Purvis is responsible for *that* girl's murder today. He also killed the girl you found at the house." He paused, his expression offering no satisfaction in saying, "This entire enterprise was his idea."

Moore killed both girls? Boggs wouldn't have put much past him. Taking bribes. Manipulating his power over those who could make sure he'd stay in office. But murder?

And then, his mind brought up the image of Sears holding up the handcuffs. Mespelt's voice stating how the City once ordered that type. Sear's discrepancy with Potter's autopsy report. He remembered both Walter and Oliver emphatically stating it was Jake's father at the hospital, but Potter denied it. What had Bill Cahill known about the place on the Summit?

He asked Moore, "What's this enterprise Cletus is talking about?"

Moore grinned. "Cletus got a little lonely after Martha died, so he and I put together a little, what you'd call, a "gentleman's club." A partnership of sorts. He supplied the place, and I got the girls." A tip of his tongue licked his bottom lip. "Sorry, we couldn't offer you a membership. But we didn't think your principals would match our mission statement."

"Evidence will eventually tie you to the crimes. And if what Cletus is saying isn't true, you'll get your ability to explain."

"Cletus's word?" Moore laughed. "You'll need more than his word. He's in this as deep as I am." His mouth grew hard, "Besides, I'll be long gone before the full story comes out."

He pointed his gun directly at Potter. "You helped me here, Cletus. I'll just empty those suitcases into your bedroom. Hang open a few drawers." He eyed Boggs, "Knowing how you like to do everything by the book, I bet you called in that you were heading here."

Moore was wrong. Boggs had turned around and headed to the hospital directly after talking to Elizabeth. And when he found Potter missing from the hospital, he came straight here. So it'd be a while before they began to wonder where he was. And by the time they followed his steps...

"This is how I picture it," Moore continued. "You came in during the robbery. Unfortunately, you both were killed. The robber escaped. No witnesses."

"There's one witness," Potter offered.

Moore's head jerked to him.

Potter said, "Bill Cahill is still alive."

"You're lying, " Moore barked.

Potter grinned.

Boggs glanced over to Potter. He was lying. Boggs wondered how Potter was going to play it.

"I don't believe you." Moore raised his gun to aim at Potter's head.

Potter's voice was calm. Maybe he knew it was his last chance to save himself. "He was alive when he got to the University Hospital. They called to let me know. If anyone can save him, UI can."

"You imbecilic moron." Moore's fired his gun.

Boggs instinctively reached for his.

"Hold that thought," Moore shouted to Boggs. "Drop it."

Thrown back by the power of the bullet piercing and crumbling his head, blood and brain matter splattered on the wall behind Potter's body.

Moore repeated, "I said drop it."

Boggs hesitated. Then he dropped his gun.

Moore glanced over to Potter.

"The fool," Moore sneered. "He never could do anything right."

CHAPTER FIFTY: OFFICER HAYWORTH

Hayworth was confused at first as to where the Sheriff was heading.

Then whose front door was he knocking on? Boggs appeared mad as hell.

Then, for a fleeting moment, Hayworth thought he saw a curtain in the front window move. He thought it looked like Chief Moore. He wasn't sure. In fact, he might be totally wrong. If Boggs was sticking his nose into the Chief's business, the Chief was going to be mad as hell.

Hells Bells. This day started as a ruin and hadn't stopped rolling downhill. Hayworth sweated out what he should do.

And then, the door opened. Dr. Potter stood in the entry.

Relief. Okay, this was Dr. Potter's house. So that explained why the Chief might be inside. But it didn't explain why Boggs charged out of the hospital parking lot with lights flaring unless the Chief was hurt. But why would the Chief be at the doctor's house instead of the hospital?

They could be gathering to discuss the girl's death. If so, Hayworth thought, none inside would want his butting in. So the only decision to make, he thought, was to turn around and head to Eagles as he'd first been doing before seeing Boggs.

He watched as Boggs went into the house. The door closed.

Hayworth waited in his cruiser until he could wait no longer, his curiosity plaguing him. You know what happened to that stupid cat, he warned himself, but still, he got out and crouched-walked over to the tall shrubbery. He pushed his way through and continued crouch-slinking next to the shrubs as if he had become a branch, moving as quickly and quietly to the window where he'd seen the curtain moved aside.

No sliver of an opening. However, he could hear voices. The Chief was saying, "We can all sit down and sort this out." The Chief's voice was most unmistakable as if he was standing the closest to the window.

Like he'd thought. The three were meeting.

Hayworth couldn't think of any other time when so much was going on, and so many questions needed answering.

He leaned forward and placed his ear onto the glass, hearing, "Purvis is *responsible for that* girl's murder today."

Hayworth jerked back from the glass as if the window was electrified.

He repeated the words responsible for *that girl's murder*. They hadn't been distinctly clear, but the immediate image of the Chief's SUV came into his mind. He felt the bulge in his pocket. The Flag pin, an exact match to the one the Chief wore, dropped to the street.

Crazy like a fool, he chastised himself. The Chief may be many things, and Hayworth never deluded himself in thinking his boss was a good defender of the law, but rape and murder?

He second-guessed himself. Or was another person in the room trying to pin the Chief for the killing? Someone else who had seen the Chief on Concord Street.

Hells-bells. That didn't make any sense either. Why would Dr. Potter, the Sheriff, and the Chief all be here at the Doc's house and the killer inside?

He had to find out.

He moved around the house, past the front door. He kept to the shadow of the building until he came to its edge. An unlatched gate offered entry to the backyard. He went through, holding his crouch until he got to the back door. A frame in the window had been broken. The door ajar.

He pushed the door open. The voices were coming from the next room.

His duty belt felt as if it'd slipped to his knees. His steps were heavy. He moved across on the balls of his feet. He put his hand to the swinging door. Just enough to open it so he could hear better. Maybe he could get a look into what was going on.

He reasoned that if he was butting in, he could kiss his sorry ass goodbye. If he...

He fell to the ground as the shot rang out.

"Drop it."

At first, Hayworth thought the voice was commanding him. His arms flew out straight above his head. His eyes clenched closed. His body froze, rigid. Then, nothing. No sign of a threat.

He waited for the sound of the next shot. Praying it wasn't for him.

When nothing happened, he dared to open his eyes. The door next to him was still closed.

"The fool. He never could do anything right."

This time, Hayworth knew who was speaking. No doubt. Had the Chief looked in to find him having foolishly fallen to a suspect's command?

When the voices continued, he picked himself up off the floor. The next voice he heard was that of Boggs'.

He lightly touched his fingers to the swinging door, to catch a glimpse of the other side.

FIFTY-ONE: SHERIFF BOGGS

Boggs studied Moore, trying to find the man he may have been if something in his life hadn't turned him so wrong.

He repeated, "You're not going to get away, Purvis. Once they tie you to this girl's murder, as well as to the girl at the house, and the kidnappings, you'll be looking over your shoulder for the rest of your life. You'll be hunted down."

And then, Boggs saw a bit of movement. A peak of light flashed beyond where Moore stood. The door. Open. Close.

"I'll be long gone," Moore said. "There're countries that don't mind harboring fugitives. I've made a list."

Boggs stayed his glance to Moore, although he caught a slight change in light when the door opened fully. It omitted a small squeak Boggs thought Purvis would surely hear. And when Purvis didn't react, Boggs gave a slight nod and readied his legs to spring as soon as Purvis's attention was distracted.

"Good try," Purvis said. "But I'm not falling for anything so obvious."

"Hold on there," a voice demanded. "What the heck is going on. Drop the gun."

Purvis jerked around.

Boggs broke his position, leaping towards Purvis. His aim on one thing only, take the gun out of a mad man's hand.

A shot rang out.

CHAPTER FIFTY-TWO

Boggs took charge of Officer Hayworth's weapon and called Rants to handle the crime scene.

Rants had trouble taking in the report. It was still surreal to Boggs, too. Were there others? Did Moore have a hand in Bill Cahill's death? From what Potter said, Boggs was reasonably sure of it. How complicit was Potter? What went on in that house up on Summit? What did Cahill know? And who else knew?

A streak of lightning severed the darkness. The sky turned a greenish-black. The storm wasn't forecasted any longer. The storm had arrived.

City Police cruisers. Forensics' van parked in Cetus Potter's driveway.

Boggs heard his radio. It was Standwick.

"I've placed Donald Goode under arrest for the accidental shooting of Phil Wilmer."

"What the hell?" Boggs responded. "How the hell did that happen?"

"He said he thought Wilmer was Ted Templeton pointing a ray gun at him."

"Keep Goode until I get there."

"Copy that."

Twenty minutes later, he pulled into the parking lot at Eagles. The AirCare stood with blades quieted. Standwick waited for him by a cruiser. Boggs got out and walked over. "What's Wilmer's condition?"

"Ambulance has already taken him into Pinkerton General. EMT said the shot went through the shoulder, but he'll be okay."

Boggs glanced to the cruiser and saw Donald Goode in the back seat. Goode dropped and turned his head quickly away.

"I heard there was a shooting at Doc Potter's place? Standwick voice was incredulous, "Moore's involved in all of this?"

Boggs held up a hand. "I'll tell you all of it, or as much as I've pieced together after we get this situation under control."

"They're all over this park." Standwick said, "According to Goode, Forester's setup at that burned house. Guess he's using it as his command for this shit-storm."

Boggs glanced back inside the cruiser, steeling his eyes on Goode. Goode might not be looking in his direction, Boggs thought, but Boggs was sure Goode could feel his disgust. The guilt showed on his reddened neck and the trembling of his hands.

"What's this ray-gun thing?" Boggs asked.

"Forester told them Templeton wasn't just a retard or killer."

Boggs cringed at the word retard but didn't interrupt.

"He convinced them he was an alien. That's where the ray gun comes in. It's like *War of the Worlds* here."

Forester's crowd was letting fiction cut out all reason.

If Donald Goode, someone who couldn't shoot a deer even though he went out hunting with his friends, could get riled up enough to shoot someone, alien or not, Boggs thought there would be a lot more accidents. Or next time, someone killed.

He demanded of Standwick, "I want arrests made, and those men pulled out of this park."

"We've arrested ten already." Standwick pointed over across the way.

The white command tent was still set up, and Boggs now saw the faces of other men he knew. Hands banded.

Standwick told him they had all been charged with recklessness at this point, and they had been told other charges could be forthcoming.

"Put the word out," Boggs said. "We caught who murdered the girl."

Standwick opened his mouth to ask who, but Boggs was determined to get the situation under control. If he couldn't, he'd need to call the State Troopers in for help.

Standwick said, "AirCare wasn't needed for Wilmer. I thought you'd want it left here. But the pilot says he has to go now or never."

Boggs answered by moving straight off for the copter. He raised his index finger and circled in the air to tell the pilot they were taking off.

As the helicopter flew towards the Summit, Boggs thought of Teddy. A young boy tormented by those who saw difference as a threat. And then the image of his sister Laura flashed in his mind. The boys who had hunted her down didn't physically hurt her, but emotional violence leaves bruises that can't be seen. Cuts that can sever the heart. Bleeding out black thoughts for any prospect of inclusion.

And he, knowing how she was treated by others, by those who didn't understand how she worked so hard to be normal, he'd done nothing. He'd hit her just as hard. Maybe even harder. He'd thrown the final punch by not letting her come into his room.

He wasn't going to let that happen to Teddy. Somehow, he would find the kid before something worse happened to him.

CHAPTER FIFTY-THREE: MAJOR SEARS

Noah left his car before the entrance and walked into Eagles Park.

He had been trying to reach Bill again mentally but heard nothing back, which led him to only one conclusion. Bill was dead.

A thunderclap resounded overhead.

Sears skirted the cruiser parked to keep others out. He hurried, crossing to the path he'd taken last. Thunder rumbled.

CHAPTER FIFTY-FOUR: JAKE CAHILL

The resounding thunder came into the cave, ricocheting off the walls.

An echo left a steady hum as if the walls absorbed the sound, and the timber of the vibration became one with the stone. Like a turning fork setting the pitch.

A low ache ballooned in Jake's head, and the middle of his forehead throbbed like a heart's quickened beat.

"*YONNNNADADDDO*"

This time Johnny's garble was more insistent. He pointed his finger at Jake.

Teddy nodded as if answering Johnny.

"We need to go," Teddy said.

Jake jumped up. The best words he'd ever heard.

And then he heard his name being called. But not by Teddy, or Johnny. Someone was standing in the darkness from the same place Teddy had come in.

SQUEAL!

From the darkness, Jake saw the best thing he could have ever hoped to see. Chewbacca came running out of the blacky ink into the circle of firelight.

CHAPTER FIFTY-FIVE: MAJOR SEARS

Noah heard the rotors of a helicopter overhead.

The wind was picking up. Whoever was coming up to the summit was risking it.

He knew there wasn't much time left. Something was happening. He'd interviewed others about something, but only had a handful of memory flashes to call his own.

He was pretty sure now he knew why Bill Cahill had called him and said *Eagles' Nest*.

He went over to where Boggs had shown him the prints. He continued beyond them, following until they vanished. He pushed through thick brush, moving by instinct.

The static in the air was rising. His forehead throbbed with pressure. His ears hummed.

He got to the gulch and, this time, continued. Then he heard a dog bark. He looked and saw a large, brown Labrador standing on a rock, tongue out, tail wagging.

Noah called. "Take me to Jake."

The dog took off.

Noah hurried to climb to the top of the rock and raced in the direction he saw the dog go. He scaled over more large rocks, grappled brush.

And then he heard his name, "Sears!"

But he didn't stop.

Not until he saw the large dog standing as if patiently waiting for him. And when Noah walked up to him, "It's okay, boy. Where's Jake?" the dog turned and slipped behind some straggled brush.

He found himself in a cave—void of light.

Thunder blasted. The booming volley rolled into the darkness, ricocheting off the walls. Echoing a path that Noah followed until he came to where the darkness lessened, and light illuminated a group sitting around a small, blazing fire.

SQUEAL!

Noah's eyes adjusted. He could see a girl and a boy. An older boy, and ...

"Good, God, what is that?" Sheriff Boggs came up to stand next to him. He had his gun out.

"Put that away," Noah ordered. He stepped toward the group.

"Sheriff Boggs," Jake called out. "Boy, it's good to see you."

Ted Templeton took off his Cardinal's hat. And when he did, Noah heard, "We need to hurry."

Another massive pounding of thunder.

Noah nodded. "Okay, you guys. Let's go." He glanced at his friend's son.

Jake's eyes were large and golden.

CHAPTER FIFTY-SIX: SHERIFF BOGGS

"What is that...an animal?"

Sears took him by the arm. "I'll explain later. We have to go."

Boggs allowed himself to be led as the group rushed back to the trail to the lake. At first, it was Sears leading, but then suddenly, the strange looking... animal, human?... moved out and around and began to lead.

SQUEAL!

The Labrador shadowing it, barking.

The storm overhead continued to roar. Streaks of brilliant light cutting through the clouds.

They stopped just above the lake. Boggs shook his head. Tried to clear his mind. The humming in his ears fuzzed his thoughts.

And then he saw a brilliant funnel of light moving out of the dark clouds.

"Sears?" Boggs called. "What the hell?"

Stunning in light. Thronging with sound.

Ted said to Sears, "It's waiting for us."

Sears nodded. "Have you gone before?"

"No," Ted told him. "But Mr. Cahill told me I would be going home someday. He explained to me what Johnny and I are. Where we came from. We're not the only ones."

And Sears nodded, agreeing.

"I'm not afraid," Ted said. "I know Johnny and I can't stay here. Not now. Maybe someday. We are too different. Maybe someday we can return when there is no difference between any of us."

Ted turned to Jake. "It's up to people like you to each the others."

Boggs saw that Jake seemed as stunned as he was in what was happening. His eyes glowed stronger. More golden.

Boggs looked for the girl? Where was the girl?

Then his attention was taken from searching for her to the funnel of brilliance at the lake's edge and a shadow of movement. More than one. Something was being pulled into the light. People.

Ted headed down. When there, he glanced back. Waved. And then, he stepped into the light.

And then Jake moved as if to follow. Boggs went to reach out to stop him but realized he had control over his arms and legs.

Instead, Sear stepped in front of Jake, stopping him. He shook his head. The two stared at each other as if communicating, but their mouths weren't moving.

Boggs continued to struggle to move. He couldn't believe what he was seeing. He couldn't believe he couldn't move, although there was nothing to restrain him.

But he also couldn't deny either one.

Jake pointed to what was happening below.

Boggs heard Sears say, "It's not your time, Jake."

Again, Boggs tried to move. Finally, yelling, "Damn it, what's holding me? What the hell do you mean, it's not his time?"

Boggs felt like he was going insane.

Another burst of thunder. A flash of lightning.

The brilliant funnel vanished.

Fire and bolts of lightning, booms of thunder.

CHAPTER FIFTY-SEVEN

Boggs woke to the sound of sirens.

Tornado.

He startled, finding himself in his SUV in the parking lot by the station. And more surprisingly, he saw Jake Cahill sitting in the passenger seat. And in back, a girl.

"What's going on?" Jake said, coming awake, too. "Where am I?"

The last thing Boggs remembered was getting into the AirCare and taking off to reach Summit before the storm broke. Two officers arresting Doug Forester at the burned house.

Then?

Suddenly, someone pounded on the glass.

Standwick. "You okay, Sheriff?"THAT

"I guess so," Boggs answered.

"I didn't think we'd get the two of you off Summit before the AirCare was grounded." He leaned over Boggs, "You okay, Jake?"

"Yeah," Jake answered. "I think so."

"What's this about AirCare?" Boggs asked.

"When we got the call that you found Jake, I told the pilot he needed to take off asTHATsoon as he could. The report was the tornado was headed straight towards us." Standwick sighed. Wiped his forehead. "When I saw that funnel flying overhead, I thought we were all were done for."

"Hold it." Standwick glanced to Jake and Boggs. "How did the two of you get here? AirCare brought down Forester. I thought you were still up on Summit. When I left the park, your SUV was still in the lot."

Then Boggs remembered. “Sears? Did Sears get back?”

Who? Standwick asked.

“Major Noah Sears?”

Standwick gave him a quizzical look. “Not sure who you’re talking about, Sheriff.”

CHAPTER FIFTY-EIGHT

Wind speeds reached 170 miles per hour.

Experts state that the odds of an E-F4 or stronger tornado hitting in the same exact place are rare. But rarity offers little consolation to a community that finds itself standing again amid the rubble of homes just dug out and considered rebuilding.

"You shouldn't have to go through this once in your lifetime, let alone twice," a Pinkerton resident told this reporter as she stood amid the debris that had been her home.

The list grows of those missing, and authorities are still unsure of the exact number of people injured.

But not only has Pinkerton experienced the tragedy of another tornado, its Chief of Police has been named as a suspect in murder and kidnapping. Acting-Commander Regis Rants, now acting-Chief of Police for Pinkerton until another Chief can be hired, offered little information stating that the investigation of Chief Moore for the suspected murder of Dr. Cletus Potter, the murder of the girl found on Concord Street, and another girl found at the summit of Eagles Park is still on-going.

Boggs laid the newspaper aside. The article told him nothing more than what he already knew, but he felt there was something beneath the words, something else that happened.

Something beneath the fog of his memory. No matter how hard he tried, he couldn't place together the time he'd lost between going out to Eagles' Park, meeting with Standwick, jumping into AirCare, then winding up back in the station's lot in his SUV with Jack Cahill and a girl.

No matter how many times he mentioned Sears to Standwick, Standwick returned he wasn't sure the two had met.

The girl had been a surprise. She, too, had little memory of what happened to her, but she did tell him about her experience at the Summit house. And, what happened to Bill Cahill.

She remembered Ted finding her. "He was a little strange looking," she'd offered. Then, she hesitated, "I think he could hear what I was thinking because sometimes he would answer my thoughts. He might not be like me, or me like him, but he could see me. Really see me." She grew silent, then said, "Maybe we should all be able to read each other's thoughts. Hear the sameness in each other even if we can't see it."

Boggs shook his head. There was a lot of truth in what she'd said.

But he would think about it later. He had more pressing matters at hand. As it turned out, she was able to implicate more people involved with Moore and Potter. Her description of Carl Hiddleson led to Hiddleson claiming Moore may have had something to do with Deputy Wilcox's death. The AirCare pilot who had brought Doug Forester back to command ended up confessing to having known and participated in what Moore had named Pointe House.

Boggs got up and was stopped as his phone rang. He picked it up.

"Sheriff Boggs? This is Jake Cahill."

"Hello, Jake. How are you doing?"

"Okay, sir."

Boggs had already heard that when Jake returned home, he'd found his mom and sister waiting. He still hadn't learned all the details about where they'd been. He expected to hear they'd been sheltered during the storm and hadn't been able to get back home until before the second storm hit.

"I'm sorry about your Dad," Boggs offered.

"Thank you. At least Dr. Potter tried to get him help."

"Is there anything I can do for you?" Boggs asked.

Jake asked, "Do you remember anything, Sheriff?" He said, "I get snatches of memory. I think I was somewhere in the dark. There was a fire like a campfire. I am pretty sure there was someone with me, although I can't see him. I am trying to piece the memories together."

"I'm just glad we found you," Boggs offered.

"I think Teddy was there, Sheriff."

Ted Templeton was on a list of those missing.

Boggs wasn't sure if either of them would ever remember all the events that took place during that storm. But he was pretty sure, whatever happened, was something so powerful his mind couldn't take in all in. Not now, at least. Maybe someday.

But other events were evident. Doug Forester was charged for inciting a riot, which led to Phil Wilmer's shooting. Several, including Donald Goode having shot Wilmer, were arrested for pursuing a boy who had no control over how he was born.

Boggs felt satisfaction in trying to help Ted Templeton. While Ted may have gotten caught by the storm, and Tira lost her son, he had wanted to keep him from the harmful discrimination of others. He wished he could have done the same for his sister. But then, you can't would of, could of, or should of in life, he acknowledged. You take on life as best as you can. What he could do, and would, make a point of keeping in touch with Tira.

"Sheriff?"

"Yes, Jake?

"Do you want to remember, Sheriff? Don't you want to learn exactly what happened to us? The truth?"

Boggs didn't reply right away. The investigator in him wanted to refollow the clues and go over everything that had occurred. But clues to what? Dr. Potter was dead. Chief Moore was under arrest and would stand trial for murder and kidnapping. Those were actual events. His time-lapse? He had made calls inquiring about a Federal Agent by the name of Noah Sears, and each inquiry came to a dead end.

"The truth is, Jake. You were lost up on Summit. And you're safe now."

An exhalation of breath came over the phone. "I will never forget," Jake said to him. "Not totally." And he added, "I don't think you will either."

He's right, Boggs thought. Someday, he hoped one of them would come up with answers to what they experienced. But what had happened was behind them. Boggs vowed now to stay as Sheriff for a few more years. He would continue to walk into the storm of disparity and crime and do what he could to make life, at least in Circlegold, better.

About Author

D. J. ADAMSON considers herself a storyteller and not just a genre author. All of her novels are suspenseful, ranging from mystery to thriller, including her science fiction novels. DJ teaches writing at Southern CA colleges, where she lives with her husband and Welsh Terrier, Maverick.

Acknowledgments

Thank you for reading *Into the Storm*. A reader should always be the first acknowledged. For without you, stories would remain silent. I always write first for my muse, because the storyteller in me won't let me rest until it is worked out and on the page. Then, I put all of my efforts into offering the reader enjoyment, sometimes thought-provoking possibilities, and I personally enjoy the process of the craft. I have had great fun writing both *Approaching Storm* and *Into the Storm*. And while some readers have speculated, or feel, a third book is required to explore what Jake Cahill realized from his experience, that decision has not yet been made. However, the title: *Storm Chaser* has been suggested to my muse.

Having only experienced a UFO sighting once in my life, or the possibility of a UFO, I have continually wanted to chase the concept that they do exist. Michio Kaku says if you are abducted, steal something. Even if it is a paperclip. You bet I would try. For, I believe in the possibility of the impossible. Life has taught me that lesson.

The first book *Approaching Storm* works as a Prologue to this book. I wrote the first draft of the entire story about twenty years ago. Stephen King said he put drafts of manuscripts in his closet. I also once read where he would take them down to a bank box. Of course, that is when Stephen King's manuscripts, drafts, and notes became valuable to anyone who could put their hand on one. Mine are safe in my closet and available when the muse decides to look at an idea for a story one more time.

Why Iowa? My family roots are there, and the area speaks to me when I visit. Also, the storms of Iowa are memorable whether large or small.

Now, to thank those who understand why I do what I do, and who encourage me to keep doing it. First, I am grateful to those who inspire and indulge my conversations on UFOs. Thanks, Shayn Adamson, Mario Alcalde, Veronica Alcalde, and the students who have taken my writing classes at Glendale College. Thank you to those who have encouraged me to continue picking up my pen: Rachelle LaPan, Laurie Stevens, Nancy Cole Silverman, Melanie Wilken, Kathy Shields, Rebecca Martinez, Liz Chang, and my author friends whose fingers tap computer keys to create literary music. I always learn from all of you. Thank you, Aaron Hudson, for keeping me spiritually grounded. And a special mention to my husband Tom who reminds me to keep my logical foot touching the earth while flying with my imagination. He has always enriched my life with his sense of adventure.

*

D.J. ADAMSON

APPROACHING STORM

www.ingramcontent.com/pod-product-compliance
Lightning Source LLC
LaVergne TN
LVHW100524110826
845146LV00002B/771
* 9 7 9 8 9 8 8 6 5 9 3 0 3 *